SOMETHING RIGHT

THE BLISSWOOD BROTHERS
BOOK 1

EVEY LYON

THE BLISSWOOD BROTHERS

Something Right

Something More

Something Good

Something Beautiful

ABOUT

It wasn't in my plan to take care of my teenage sister, but with our parents now gone, I move back to the town I left 12 years ago to do just that. My sister is full of attitude and doesn't miss the opportunity to remind me that I've traded off my corporate office for small-town antics or that Brooke Rivers, of all women, is living next door with an adorable three-year-old kid who may just wrap me around her finger— the kid, I mean... okay, the mom too.

But it's complicated.

It involves a weekend way back, in a bed Brooke and I never left—the memory of me hurting her, and the moment Brooke got her chance to hurt me too. In her head, she's built a giant wall between us. In my mind, I'm determined to tear it down. And as luck would have it, I need her cookies for the high school bake sale, and she needs my skills at putting together her daughter's new playhouse. Soon we are exchanging favors, and even better, our clothes are ending up on the floor in the process.

But she's adamant that there is too much at stake for us.

And when a twist of fate hits us, unexpectedly revealing a secret, I'm beginning to think that she may be right, or just maybe, what she and I have may finally be something right...

GRAYSON

I've got this. She can't undermine me. Not if I do it first. No, I've totally got this. I'll play it cool and relatable before laying the ground rules for who's in charge. Here we go…

I slide my eyes up to study my sister Lucy sitting behind the island in the kitchen. As I push the empty pizza box to the side, I make a note in my head that I should do a grocery run later, as cold pizza for lunch is getting repetitive. Unfortunately, grocery delivery isn't an option in this town.

"Stop staring at me, Grayson." Lucy glares up from her bright orange nails typing away on her phone—the phone I want to throw against a wall most days. Her brown hair is up in a high ponytail, so I have a full view of her unimpressed look, and I know a sarcastic remark will be coming at me in the next thirty seconds.

It's been two weeks since I moved into my father's home that he bought a few years back so that Lucy could be closer to school. The home I never planned to live in. No, I planned to live in my overpriced apartment in Chicago enjoying after-work drinks at up-and-coming hotspots across the city.

Instead, there is a solid path of cornfields between suburban life and the nature of rural Illinois. And I am on the wrong side of the path, in Bluetop, the quirky small town that for some reason draws people to stop rather than just passing through.

"All homework done for tomorrow?" I dare to ask, and her eyeroll tells me that I'm an idiot for expecting an answer from a sixteen-year-old.

I was thirteen when Lucy was born. Considering my two brothers are only slightly younger than me, it was always assumed that Lucy was a surprise for our parents. Despite our mother passing at birth, Lucy was a light in the family, and she automatically gained three older brothers who would protect her to no end.

She never knew our mother, so her death never affected Lucy the same way that it did us. But when our father passed a month ago from cancer, she continued on as if it was normal. Maybe it was the fact that we'd all had a year to prepare for it, but her resilience still amazes me, just like I accepted the timing of our dad's passing as the way it was somehow supposed to be.

"Look, Lucy, I don't enjoy having to play the uncool brother, but you're a smart kid, and we need to start thinking about college." I hate myself right now. I'll be reflecting on my choice of words later with a cold beer in hand.

Her nails tap the counter in a firm beat. "Relax. I know you were the one nominated against your will to take care of me, so you don't need to be such a martyr."

I smirk at her viewpoint. "You really need to stop refer-ring to me as a martyr, or at least actually look up the meaning of the word and use it in a correct context."

"Take a chill pill, Grays." She stares at me as I cross my

arms and lean against the fridge. Huffing out a breath, she finally answers me. "Homework is done, and I would appreciate if we kept college talk to school hours. I need *me time* during the evenings and weekends. We would hate for you to be the reason that it's ruined." Her mocking tone tells me she believes her philosophy.

I shake my head at her *me time* reasoning that she has thrown at me on multiple occasions now.

Fuck, I could use some *me time*. This whole situation has my head spinning. I swear my father is up there laughing at how he got me back to Bluetop. In a last-minute change to his will, Jack Blisswood, dear old dad, chose me to be guardian of Lucy, when there are two other brothers who are more than capable—wait, I know why. Because everyone perceives me as the responsible one because my two brothers still throw down like they're eighteen and break hearts like it's part of a daily routine.

But the real reason is my father wanted to strongarm me into being more involved in the family business—Olive Owl.

And Olive Owl is something special. It's a farm and vineyard, the full package, with a restaurant and bed-and-breakfast. Hell, I have friends from the city who head out here just to stay at Olive Owl. We are a good middle point between Wisconsin, the Tri-Cities to the west, and suburban Chicago. The produce is delicious, the scarce Midwest wine award-winning, and I'm sure even the cows would sing our praise.

But I never had interest in running the place. I'm an architect, an excellent one. To my father's dismay, I opted not to play college ball and went straight into my degree. I left for the city life, and I got it… only to have to retreat.

The deep sigh from my sister has me widening my eyes in curiosity. "What is it now?"

"My phone battery died."

"Ooh, that's a travesty," I retort.

"It is. Kendall was telling me about this party next week. Can I go?" I hear the hope in her tone.

The thing about our situation is I am too young to be in a father role to a teenager, as it feels like just yesterday when I was her age. Shit, my brothers and I got up to stuff when we were her age too. I know every trick she is going to try and pull, because I wrote the fucking book. That's how I know that even if I say no, she will make it her mission to go.

And considering everything she's been through, the spark of happiness flashing across her face for hanging out with her friends is a welcome change. She has a strong mind, she spends more than enough time tending to her horse, and she would rather read a book than chase after boys.

…Wait a second. Now that I reflect on my image of her and the fact no sixteen-year-old is that immune to hormones and first love, I know it can't be all that it seems. But one day at a time, and thankfully, the message is clear in town that Lucy has three brothers with a good left hook.

Which is why I say, "If you tell me where and when, don't get into trouble between now and then, and you follow the rules."

"I know, I know. If there's drinking, call you no matter the time to pick me up so I don't go in anyone's car."

I nod and feel like we can meet in the middle on this. It's a relief, since I'm not in the mood to debate. Heading to the dishwasher, I begin to put the dishes in.

"Bennett said he'll help me practice driving this afternoon since you can't stomach me behind a wheel," Lucy reminds me, and I'm happy my brother is taking responsibility for the 'get our kid sister her driving license' project.

"I know, and I will stay off the road," I tease my sister.

"Ha, ha."

Bennett and Knox live at Olive Owl. Knox, the youngest of my brothers, has been running the operations of the place since day one of adulthood; it's more his than ours. Bennett is closest to my age and took on running the business side of things. Yet we all have an equal share, so we try to pitch in when we can.

As I focus on the dishes, I can hear Lucy putting her phone on the charger. Glancing out the kitchen window to the gray spring day, that tightening around my chest hits me. The house next door may be the most unplanned thing in all of this.

My sister comes to my side to pick up a sponge, which surprises me. Normally, I need to ask her three times to help clean up the kitchen.

But the moment she opens her mouth, I realize it's too good to be true.

"Brooke and Rosie come back today from visiting her grandparents," she reminds me, and she flashes her eyes at me.

Just the sound of her name causes a thrum somewhere within me.

"And?"

"You can't avoid her forever."

I shake my head to myself. "I'm not avoiding her, she just happened to be away since I moved back."

My upper lip twitches from the thought of seeing Brooke again. Back in high school, she was the cheerleader every guy wanted. I was the lucky one to call her mine. Christ, she could bend like no other too. Being with her was a dream... until we imploded.

"Don't screw it up. Brooke is really cool. She lets me

babysit Rosie, and I need Brooke happy so she can teach me her pasta recipe since I can't keep eating pizza."

"You don't know anything about it, Lucy," I state, as I'm not sure what Lucy would understand about my romantic history.

"Please," she sneers. "Your homecoming king and queen photo hits my eye sockets every day on entering the school. I know you two had a thing."

A *thing* is an understatement.

First love, inseparable days, unrealistic plans of a future that were too good to be true. Her caramel-brown hair wrapped around my hands and her blue eyes bright with love for me.

A *thing* doesn't even cover the surface.

"Doesn't matter." I hear the somber in my tone.

It's been four years since I last saw her, in the only way we know; her under me with her eyes piercing me, asking me for something more. Again in our twenties, we reconnected for an instant and acted like two insatiable people clueless to the impossibility of a future.

"Well, figure it out, because her car just pulled up and we have a casserole dish to return. I'm not doing it, so you have fun with *that* situation." The satisfied look my sister gives me tells me she's enjoying this.

Looking out the window to the driveway next door, I see the small blue SUV park, and I know my time has come.

But that's the thing—I'm ready, or at least I think I am.

Because Brooke Rivers is the only woman who I would want to make squirm again. Who, despite the way last time went down—and hell, that was a rollercoaster of crazy—I still can't keep her out of my mind.

And if there is anything about my new way of life that I can't try to avoid, it's the complication of running into my ex, because it's just impossible to avoid one another in this town.

"Don't do anything I would do," I say as I move to leave and see that Lucy has conveniently grabbed the dish for me while I was thinking about the hundred ways this all could go.

"Me? I'm perfectly behaved." Her sentence is dripping with sarcasm as she holds up the glass oven dish.

I gently pull her ponytail before taking the dish.

Heading out through the garage, I'm thankful that my dark long-sleeve shirt and jeans are the right outfit for running into your ex. As my feet begin to walk in the direction of her driveway, my adrenaline spikes, because her silhouette alone does something to me.

Her sunglasses are on top of her head, her hair down well past her shoulders in natural waves. Her jeans are a perfect fit, showing me the curve of her ass that I want to squeeze, and an olive-green sweater that brings out the blue in her eyes, with her lashes fluttering.

My worst fear.

She gets more fucking beautiful as time passes. Her glow is different from when we last saw one another, only better, more gentle, pure radiance.

Our eyes meet, her pink lips part, and her breath cuts as she stops in her tracks.

God, I hope her mouth curves up into a smile.

"You knew this was coming." I have to offer her a gentle grin.

Her face is frozen, but inside I'm screaming, *Smile for me, you know you want to.*

"Grayson…" she begins, but the squeal of a tiny human in the car breaks our locked gaze.

A reminder that we are two very different people now.

That pinch in my stomach reminds me that she's a mom,

and I'm the guy who broke her heart over reasons that are no
longer valid.

"You really want to do this reunion now?" She breathes
out, and I hear half-amusement, half-annoyance in her tone.

"Yeah. Yeah, I do."

2

GRAYSON

"Mommy, Mommy!" The sound of a little girl distracts us, and Brooke immediately heads to the backseat door, glancing over her shoulder at me, unsure maybe.

Opening the door, she soothes the child. "We're home. Let's get you out of this car seat, huh?"

I can't help but be mesmerized by the scene in front of me. The way Brooke softly smiles and tickles her daughter before lifting her out of the seat and bringing the little girl to stand on the driveway.

It takes only a second for the little human to appear at my feet, peering up in wonder. There's a unicorn stuffed animal hanging from her hand, and her bright blue eyes are staring at me, wide. The spitting image of Brooke.

"Rosie, this is Grayson. He is Lucy's oldest brother… and… our neighbor," Brooke says hesitantly as she tucks a strand of hair behind her ear.

Neighbor, huh. Not sure I like that title.

Kneeling down, I come eye to eye with the toothy kid

with brown pigtails. "Hey there, I'm Grays. How old are you?" A silly question, as her age is drilled into my brain.

Because what happened four years ago is hard to forget.

———

LOOKING across the patio of the farmhouse—now bed-and-breakfast—a sense of pride washes over me as I take a glass of white wine in my hand. The green fields contrast the orange setting sun and the sound of people chatting over wine as a trio of guitars and a simple drum play. Mason-jar lights hang over the stoned patio, and everything feels like it jumped off the page of a magazine—elegant, classy, and rustic.

My father has a permanent smile as he speaks to the mayor of Bluetop, and he gestures his hand to the barn that houses the barrels of wine. Darting my eyes to another corner, I see my brother Bennett sweet-talking a couple into who knows what, while Knox seems to be surveying the table that has snacks of our Olive Owl produce.

I haven't been back since my first year of college, but I wouldn't miss the grand opening of the bed-and-breakfast at Olive Owl. My designs helped create the expansion of the farmhouse, and I am proud of everything my family has done.

I may be trapped in a bubble of work and essential social gatherings in the city, but I praise Olive Owl at every chance I get, just like everyone in town celebrates us when we bring out a new wine, a new flavor of olive oil, or when pumpkin season starts. It's why everyone seems to be here tonight, including Brooke, who I last saw when I was home on spring break from college.

Leave it to my brothers to remain good friends with my

first love. Hell, if we were on a sinking ship, I'm sure they would choose to save Brooke over me. Not many people wouldn't.

I scan the party, knowing she's here somewhere. I somehow felt it already, anticipation runs through me. Drinking from my glass, the yearning can't be tamed. I want to speak with her and know that she's okay. Knox mentioned she broke up with someone about a month ago. She's here alone, and that's enough for my inner restraint level to reach zero.

Brooke is easy to spot because nobody else really holds a candle to her. There she is. Next to the wine table, looking around the room. Maybe she's waiting for me, because we both know tonight is a run-in that's been a long time coming.

Her peach-colored dress accentuates the small curve of her back that I used to trace with my hands. She's the perfect sweet package.

As she sips from her glass, her eyes catch me, and that's it. Nothing else tonight matters.

Tipping my glass to her from across the party, I toast her with a wink.

Her smile is an invitation to come closer.

I re-button my blazer as I walk across the patio and drink in the fact that it may be seven years later but she hasn't changed.

Arriving in front of her, we both look at one another, almost giddy.

"It's good to see you, B."

"Yeah, it's been a while."

Offering open arms, I study her to see if it's the right move. "I think we're overdue for one of these." She nods with her sweet look, and she steps into my embrace.

We went our separate paths. But here we are now, and we can't deny that it feels right.

Her fruity smell in her hair makes me dizzy for a few seconds as I get stuck in nostalgia. Tightening my arms around her, I'm surprised at how much this ignites something in me, and her hand circling on my back indicates she feels it too.

Pulling away, we make small talk for a few minutes about my upcoming promotion at work—I've been assigned a new architecture project. She tells me about nursing and some crazy ER stories, but quick pleasantries won't cut it.

I need more. More time. More of her.

"Did you have the tour?"

She licks her lips, and she knows I am about to offer to lead the way. A dangerous offer too.

"Let me guess, you'll give me the VIP version." She gives me a knowing look.

I reach out to touch her arm with my hand. "I like your thinking."

"What does the tour involve?" she curiously inquires.

I step closer to her, causing our arms to brush one another, and I lean in to let my mouth dance with her ear. My voice lowers enough to make her shudder.

"We get out of here and go for a walk."

"Okay, then what?"

I begin to circle her slowly. "We sit somewhere and catch up."

She seems to contemplate my words. "Harmless, I suppose."

"Come on, B, it's been a few years, and now that I know you're here, I won't be able to focus until I hear what you're up to. Telling you to grip the headboard is an optional activity." I nod my head in the direction of the

*door as I give her that enticing look that I feel I'm a
master at.*

Offering my hand, she takes it.

———

ROSIE HOLDS up three little fingers to indicate her age, and it
breaks me out of my memory.

I'm still kneeling down at eye level with her, but she
grows shy and holds onto Brooke's thigh and ducks behind
her mother's long legs that I have enjoyed wrapped around
my body many times.

Shy I am not. I peer up, still kneeling, with a cunning
grin. "You can still get me on my knees, B." There's a slight
playful firmness in my voice.

Brooke gives me a strained, tight-lipped smile as her long
lashes flutter. "Rosie, why don't you go grab the mail from
the mailbox. I'll watch you from here, okay?"

When the child runs down the driveway in Brooke's view,
I return to standing and wait for Brooke to lay it on me.
Because I can tell she's debating what to say or do.

Instead, she remains delicate with our interaction. "I'm
sorry about your father," she begins.

"Yeah." I scratch the back of my neck. We had a small
intimate funeral, so the town instead brought condolences in
the form of casseroles. I won't want to see green beans again
for a while, that's for sure. "Thanks for the food. I hear you
dropped some off before I got back."

"Least I could do. Lucy is great, babysits sometimes for
Rosie. Obviously, I still see Bennett and Knox a lot too."

"Right…" It trails for a few seconds as I recall how she's
friends with them both. I nod in understanding. "So, you're
living here." It comes out awkward.

So awkward that it finally causes that smile of hers to spread. "Yeah. My parents let me stay here since they moved down to Texas a few years ago. They didn't want to sell yet."

I already know this. The last few years, I've only come back on rare occasions but always to Olive Owl, which is twenty minutes out of town. Our paths never seemed to cross.

"And yep, that means we're neighbors now," she says frankly .

I chuckle just as Rosie comes plodding back with mail between her hands and a trail of envelopes on the ground behind her.

"Awesome job. You are such a great helper," Brooke praises her daughter.

Damn, Brooke is a mom. She looks like a natural too.

"I may need to hire her," I say and quickly scoop up the envelopes that Rosie has no clue she dropped.

Rosie smiles at me shyly before hiding behind Brooke's legs again. This kid is adorable.

"I think she's taking a liking to you," Brooke admits and nearly blushes in the process.

"Probably. Like mother, like daughter, or something like that."

Brooke rolls her eyes at my comment then notices the square dish. "What's that in your hand?"

Glancing down, I remember, and I hold it out to her. "Lucy mentioned this is yours."

Brooke's mouth forms a half smile, almost amused. "Wow, you are in for a ride."

Now I have to give her an entertained look. "What do you mean?"

"Considering I gave pie in a disposable dish, I am going to take a wild guess that Lucy set you up."

In this moment, I love my sister even more. Under her

sassy teenage angst is a girl who's looking out for her older brother, trying to give me an extra nudge. But I might as well use this to my advantage.

"Of course she did," I mutter and flex my jaw.

"Look, I should get Rosie inside for a snack. It was... I... Thanks for stopping by." She struggles to sew words together.

"Oh, yeah. Uhm... hey, this isn't going to be a problem, right? Me back, living next door, running into one another?"

She laughs nervously. "We have no other option. We're neighbors... It's fine. It will be fine." Her daughter begins to tug her away with impatience.

"Good," I nod gently.

"Good," she confirms and returns the similarly lost look. "Well, I should go..."

"Sure."

We struggle to break our gaze until our eyes reluctantly part. My dick is feeling an unwillingness to part too.

"See you around, Rosie." I wave to the kid.

She waves back to me. "Bye-bye."

As I turn to leave, the memory replays in my head.

———

"DON'T YOU MISS THIS, Grays? The sound of frogs and crickets at night? The smell of fresh plants mixed with horses? Everyone happy that you're here?"

It's now dark out, but the light from the party highlights her face. She's content and exactly where she wants to be in life.

"Haven't had much chance to think about it. I've been busy. Today, instead of being able to focus on helping my brothers, all I could think about is how this encounter would go. How I wanted it to go," I answer honestly.

She stops walking and waits for our bodies to face one another. "I think it's going quite okay. Kind of wish we did it sooner."

"Kind of been busy."

"I know. The ladies in the café gushed over your article about the library design in that magazine for weeks."

I quirk my mouth out at her reference as I open the back door to the bed-and-breakfast.

"Thanks for the tour." Brooke begins to take my blazer off; I still enjoy how my clothes look on her, and she was cold.

"Don't want to see the last part?" Disappointment seeps through my question as I indicate with my head to the upstairs guestrooms. I know I'm about to be greedy, but my curiosity swells when she's around, and I'm staying in one of the rooms.

Her lips tug. "I'm too scared of what could happen. Should it feel this, I don't know, normal? As if no time has passed?"

I lean against the wall. "We didn't break up because of some big event, we just grew apart."

She doesn't answer, but her head subtly nods in acknowledgment.

"I have to head back to Chicago tomorrow afternoon, I have a flight to Dallas I need to catch. But tonight... I'm not going anywhere, and even if you walk away now, you won't be leaving my bed. You will be right there, stuck in my mind as I toss and turn."

She licks her lips as a smile forms. "Those are some smooth words, Grayson Blisswood."

"Nah, it's the truth. Call me selfish, but it feels like you could still be mine, and tonight I feel like you belong to me."

Brooke steps closer to me and our hands interlink. She stares at our fingers entangled together, knotting us as one.

"Is this our closure?"

Closing our distance, my other arms pulls her flush to me. "No, B, I'm not sure closure is ever in our cards," I tell her before my lips slam down onto hers.

———

CLOSURE ISN'T FOR US, and that's why it hits me how ridiculous this is. There should be no hesitancy.

I pivot back. "Brooke," I call out, and it surprises her; I know because I notice her chest visibly moving up and down. "Coffee or dinner. You and me. That's going to happen," I inform her with confidence.

She looks away briefly. "That's not... I don't know."

"What do you have to lose?" I reaffirm, with our eyes holding in a tense stare.

I turn to walk away, but this time she's the one stopping me.

"Fine. Okay," she blurts out.

I wait for her to continue.

"Come back tonight after I get Rosie to bed?"

Slowly I nod my head in agreement. "Sounds good. Want me to bring a bottle of white?"

She scoffs a laugh and a unique look flashes across her face. "That's not what we're doing."

"What? Catching up to make this all less awkward? Or were you thinking something else..." I cock a brow at her.

Shaking her head, she guides Rosie back toward the house. "Ripping the band-aid off, that's what we're doing," she calls back to remind me.

As I turn to head back to my house, I already sense that

familiar feeling coming over me. A curiosity too overpower-ing, a fixed want that never fades, a brief whisper of a fantasy not ours.

And that uneasy feeling hitting me is a pure fact. She and I are a circle, there is no out. And this time around is no exception.

3

BROOKE

S

moothing a hand over the fabric, I study my sweater choice in the mirror. Pale blue, off-the-shoulder, with dark fitted jeans. It may seem like an easy choice, but I don't want to look like I've put much thought into this, when in fact I know this sweater brings out my eyes and my pants show off my slim body. My nails are the color of "lake house gray," whatever the hell that means, but that's the name on the bottle. I live for nail polish; otherwise, I feel naked.

It's been a few hours and my run-in earlier hasn't left my head. Grayson Blisswood is back and living next door. He's always lingered in my head, and since news broke of his return, he has fully occupied my mind.

"You can't ignore him. It's just not possible now." Kelsey throws a magazine across my bed before she grabs her blonde hair and pulls it to the side. I called her right away after Grayson left. She's been my best friend since childhood and moved back a year ago.

Nervously, I straighten the pillows on my bed. I've done my best to make this house feel more my own than my parents' over the last few years, since they're living out of state on a work assignment. The subdivision was built fifteen years ago, and all the houses on this street have the same feel and one of the three layouts.

"I know, it's fine. I'll get used to this. It's just weird, you know?" I throw myself onto the bed with a huff and try to make sense of how to feel, especially with our history.

"It doesn't have to be. You're both adults with responsibilities." She chortles a laugh. "Man, he's taking care of his sister? I couldn't imagine one of the Blisswood guys being responsible for a teenager."

"Tell me about it. But I'm sure they'll be okay. Anyhow, I wrapped my head around the fact that he and I will probably talk about what happened last time around. It's just… it feels like he doesn't hold anything against me."

Instead, his eyes feel like they're undressing me, and my body informs me it would willingly participate.

Kelsey looks at me, confused. "Why should he? You didn't do anything wrong. I know you wanted it another way. I bet he knows it too, and he won't hold it against Rosie. As much as the Blisswood brothers can be trouble, they aren't complete assholes."

That is true. Everyone knows those men are something special. Strong-headed, rugged when needed, and they clean up nicely if you throw a dress shirt at them. They are the reason women in this town have a hard time thinking clearly sometimes. Even old Mrs. Smith blushes when they walk by.

"Besides, maybe he can help you. Since you live next door to one another, it would be so easy to sneak around for a quickie."

"Kelsey!"

"What? He's single, you're single. You both have a lot going on and may need a release. And it's no coincidence that

I have been watching you fret over a shirt for twenty minutes."

I shake my head. "I have my daughter to think about, and I'm not going to add confusion to her life. Can we change the topic, please?" I plead.

She chuckles as she stands. "Actually, I should head out. I believe you have a very important guest who will probably appreciate that new bra I saw you put on." Her eyes give me a look of inquisition that causes me to grumble in response as I follow her out.

"Don't be like that. I know you still flash back to all those nights with him, that constant state of *bliss* due to his *wood*," she says in jest, and I hate her corny joke.

"I should never have called you over for a talk, you are the worst," I respond with a loving smirk.

"No, the worst would be informing you that everyone at the salon is talking about the fact Grayson is back and that they will bribe me for intel about you two." Kelsey owns a salon and is always up to date on the town gossip.

What scares me is I know she isn't joking, which only causes me to sigh as we reach the front door in this ranch-style home.

"Want to go to Rooster Sin on Friday for a drink?" she asks. The dive bar is a local institution and guaranteed good time.

"I would love to, but I would need to find a sitter. I can check with Lucy but..." I grip my neck and roll my head in slight aggravation.

Kelsey grins at me, as she's figured out my train of thought. "But then her brother would know where you are and perhaps casually drop by?"

"The last thing I need is to be around him when alcohol is involved," I admit.

As if on cue, we open the door to find Grayson on the other side... with a bottle of wine in hand and a smoldering look fit for a photoshoot.

Kelsey's face turns bright as she assesses my visitor. "Oh, look at that." She steps forward and pats his shoulder. "Right on time, as I am off. Nice touch with the family brand." Her head tilts in the direction of the Olive Owl wine he's holding in his hand.

"I see you're still around," Grayson states with feigned annoyance and that grin of his slapped across his face, only illuminated by the porch light.

"Not everyone avoids Bluetop, Grays. Anyhow, call me later, Brooke." Kelsey gives Grayson a warning glare before offering me a look that tells me good luck.

We both watch her walk away, as if we're stalling. Only when she is halfway to her car do I refocus my attention on the man in front of me. Square jaw, light brown hair the perfect length, a thin layer of scruff which only highlights the outline of his face, and eyes dark. Those eyes that twinkle with the right light. The eyes that can seep through my veins and turns me to liquid in seconds.

And here he is standing in front of me.

It's kind of funny. As a teenager, he rarely came to our front door, instead opting to climb through my bedroom window or waiting in his truck around the corner. He honestly got along just fine with my parents, but it felt like he never wanted to waste a minute and talking with my parents would drag away from our time together.

Grays is a year older than me, so when college came, we parted, since he got into his dream pick on the west coast. The summer before he left it became clear that long-distance wouldn't work. Grays wanted to get away from Bluetop and to never look back. He had a peculiar relationship with his father. Nothing crazy, just two men who didn't feel a need to be close.

The breakup in a way was easy at the end of that summer. I never even let him finish his sentence, just nodded in understanding. What hurt the most was that I was never part of any of his dream plans. And still, all my senior year of high school, I thought of him, and when he came back on winter and spring break, I fell into his arms willingly. No labels, just us. Then again my first year of college too.

My thoughts break when I hear him clear his throat.

"Right. Uhm, want to come in?"

The corner of his mouth curves up. "Kind of how these things go."

I nod in agreement and wait patiently for him to walk past me. My eyes stay glued on him as I close the door.

He knows his way around, so he walks straight to the right to the living room, his woodsy scent leaving a trail that heightens my already-sensitive senses.

"I brought a bottle of white, Olive Owl, of course." He holds up the bottle.

I bite my bottom lip and laugh softly under my breath. "I think I'll hold off on alcohol for now. Maybe lemonade?" There's a slight uneasiness to my voice.

He chuckles as if he knows my logic. "Sure. That works."

I nod—shyly, I admit—and walk to the kitchen which is off the living room. As he grabs a seat at the kitchen island, I feel a bundle of nerves inside me. The coolness from the fridge when I open the door is a welcome re-stabilizer for my body and mind.

"Rosie's asleep?"

I close the fridge with a pitcher now in my hand. I appreciate how he's slowly easing into this conversation.

"Out like a log. It was a bit of a drive from Green Bay,

but she was a trooper all the way." I can't help but gush over my daughter because she is the sweetest little nugget with such a kind heart.

"That's good. Your grandparents still don't want to leave Midwest winters?" Grayson asks as I hand him a glass.

"Nah. My parents try to convince them to move to Texas all the time, to no avail."

I sit next to him on a stool and his presence so close is like a match sparking. Maybe he feels it too, as he glances away, as if he needs to calm himself in this situation.

He angles his head and his eyes narrow. "She's a little artist." He smiles affectionately.

Looking in the direction of his sightline, I see the finger-paint and crayon drawings on the fridge. It's hard to choose one to display, so I have a fridge full of about twenty different pictures, since no mother wants to throw away their child's artwork. Every one is a little masterpiece.

"Yeah, she is. She's into baking too."

Grays looks at me with a subtle wicked smile. "You're still into art?"

I know what he's doing. A trip down memory lane. We met at the end of my sophomore year of high school in art class. I took it because I thought it would be easy, and he took it because he actually has design skills. Everyone knew who each other was, as our school wasn't that big, but one acci-dental run-in at the paintbrush sink and that's how we began.

"Never was that good at it, which is a shame, as I would love to be creative for her. You know, I always assumed you took art because baseball players were looking for the easy grades. But you actually have talent. How are you going to work from here?" I wonder, as four years ago he got a big promotion that set him in the big leagues of architecture, and he traveled all the time for work.

He sets his glass down. "I'm finishing up with a few clients online. In a few months, I need to assess my game plan. I mean, I could try working remotely since it's all temporary until Lucy is off to college, but until then, I'm here. It was part of the terms my father set out."

That thought makes my stomach curl, probably from disappointment. "Oh? Your move is temporary?"

Grays shrugs a shoulder. "I can't say. All options are on the table. How's work?"

"Not exciting," I admit, and I feel like I have nothing to brag about compared to him. "Hospital administration isn't what I had planned, but I work hours around Rosie's schedule, and the hospital has good benefits, plus the preschool is near there."

In a different life, I was an ER nurse at the regional hospital. Then I got pregnant and stopped nursing all together. The shift schedule alone was a struggle, and I just wanted a structured day for Rosie and me.

A silence takes over, and I recall the last time I saw him.

All the thoughts hit me, and a feeling of my blood racing overpowers me. I nervously fumble with the edges of my sleeves.

He smiles to himself. "Breathe. You're overthinking."

I roll my eyes, as he's right, and he knows it. Then he touches my arm, and our eyes meet.

It's so warm. It's so heartbreaking. It's so fucking hopeful, and I hate this.

"So, I believe my words were 'gripping the headboard is an optional activity'…" He has no qualms for taking an uneasy situation and making it more awkward, but it causes me to chortle.

"They were." I shift on the seat so we can face one another, and the memory flashes in my head.

I shake my head at the thought, only to realize that Grayson is watching me.

"Remembering breakfast in bed too?"

Gently, I shake my head. I do remember, every minute of it.

But I'm not going to talk about the way we caught up and talked for hours or went over memories from when we were teenagers. Or the fact that he held me like we could have a future as two adults. Any hopes that it wasn't a temporary fling went out the window when he packed up his bag and had to rush back to the city for a flight for work, and he kissed me tenderly goodbye, making it clear that was where his life was.

He has my full attention now, even more heightened when his fingertips circle the back of my hand resting on the counter.

I huff out a breath and feel the need to be bold. "This is probably when we get into the whole 'I called you a few weeks later to tell you I was pregnant with another man's baby' recap. So, I think I am going to change my policy on the wine." My tone has a little bite to it.

Sliding off my chair, I head to the cupboard to grab two wine glasses, only to finally assess him and the fixed yet subtle humored quirk of his lips.

"Wine is probably a good idea," he adds.

Bad luck or fate decided to be cruel. That's the only explanation for what happened.

Returning to him, I tip my head in the direction of the couch, and he follows. Getting settled on the sofa, we each take a sip of the dry white, which I must say, Olive Owl must've had a good year, as the wine is a perfect combination of crisp yet with a hint of fruit.

"I think I said, 'Grays, you may hear that I'm pregnant,

but don't worry, it's not yours because I'm too far along.' And we haven't spoken since, right?" I drink from my glass and decide to own all the uncomfortable details of that situation.

He nods slowly in agreement. "Yeah, it does ring a bell."

I hoped and prayed when I went into the first ultrasound that this was fate's sign for Grayson and me, only to be told how far along I was. I cried the entire appointment for so many reasons. Then the ultrasound made fresh tears burst because I fell instantly in love with the little human inside me.

"Rosie's dad?" I can see he isn't sure how to ask as he props an arm against the back of the couch.

"He signed away his rights and never met her. Can't say I even know what he's up to, as I haven't spoken to Adam since then. It's his loss not to know Rosie." Disappointment seeps through my words. He lived a few towns over, and we had met at a festival. I felt relief that he wanted no part of my life but also anger that he wanted nothing to do with his biological child. Yet if anyone could be respectable about giving up parental rights then it was him, as he was only being honest about what he wanted.

"You're doing well, B." The softness in Grays' tone causes me to slide my eyes up into his direction.

"How would you know?"

"It's Bluetop and I'm a Blisswood. My rare occasions to the grocery store are a bombardment of updates about you from every person I meet in the cereal aisle, and my brothers have made a point to bring you into daily conversation."

A smirk plays on my mouth. "Sounds about right."

My head scans the unusually clean living room floor, with toys all in their correct boxes. I spent a good thirty minutes cleaning up before my equally long sweater-choice session.

The feeling of his hand tentatively touching my arm has

me instantly melting. My eyes dart to the view of him connected to me through limbs.

"Now… we're neighbors," he almost teases.

"Yep. Look, can we just not make it complicated between us? We can be cordial, and I guess, well… cordial. That's all we need to do, nothing more." I don't have any other game-plan for this situation and instead take another sip of wine.

He circles the liquid in his glass. "Do you cordially have wine with all of your neighbors? Mr. Bigsly on the corner of the street? Because I would say we have already moved past cordial. Or are you not enjoying wine with me?" He cocks an eyebrow at me as he rubs warmth into my arm.

"Let's just agree, the occasional asking your neighbor for milk and hello on the driveway is our limit," I suggest, and he looks at me a hundred percent doubtful.

"You're going to break my sister's heart. She's thinks you're amazing and even mentioned you've been throwing on your cheerleading outfit that we all loved back in the day."

How is this possible? We went from a discussion about what went down between us to Grayson… flirting with me?

I smile to myself and snap my arm away from him. "Your sister isn't part of the complication."

"Lucky her."

My palm goes out to stop him from imagining any inac-curate facts. "I have not and will not wear my old cheer-leading outfit. I'm only helping out the girls since their coach is pregnant."

His grin spreads. "Thanks for that correction."

I can't help it, but an old habit comes over me and I play-fully slap his arm.

"Ouch. Okay, this is probably my cue to leave and check that Lucy hasn't snuck out of the house." He slowly stands with a beaming smile on his face.

"Is that a problem?"

"I don't know, I'm only two weeks in. I have just accepted that all teenage shenanigans are on the table."

Following him to set the wine glasses on the counter, I have to admire his willingness to take on the role of guardian.

"If she has her brothers' genes then for sure it's not going to be a breeze. But Lucy is a good kid and resilient too. She may just be the one chaperoning you three," I say as I open the front door.

"Since I have neighbor like you, then yeah, she may need to ground me a few times."

And fuck me, why does he have to lean against the inner door panel as he says that, with his look hot enough to start fires? A sexy smirk on display and… what? Is his shirt tugging along his chest? Because there is muscle definition happening.

Snickering under my breath, I brush past his quip. "Right. Anyhow, thanks for this chat." In a move that surprises me, I offer him my hand for a shake because I have lost all thought.

Immediately, he takes my hand and pulls me to him, causing me to instantly sink into his arms which wrap around me for a hug.

Platonic or not, I haven't been held like this by a man in years. I've missed it, but I've missed his presence perhaps even more.

We stay in an embrace for a good hot minute before parting. The back of his knuckles gently slide along my cheek as a parting move. I know this is our starting point for yet another chapter in our relationship, whatever definition it may be.

Grayson takes a few steps onto the porch then pauses before turning back to me.

"If it's any consolation, I wish the way things happened last time went differently."

His words hit me where it hurts. It could mean so many things, those words, and my heart feels like it belongs to him; it's a moment of confirmation.

Looking off into the distance, I swallow a breath. "Me too."

He lingers a few seconds longer than necessary before leaving. After watching him walk off, I close the door and collapse against the wood from slight exhaustion.

Rosie is my priority. My days of flings are long gone, and though my heart clings to a fantasy, I'm too strong to falter. Even when the feeling in the pit of my stomach reminds me of the secret wish that I harbor alone, I know I can do this.

But I can't help but wonder why fate had to make Grayson Blisswood my new neighbor. Because he knows every path to my bedroom window, and just like when we were teenagers, he still has the ability to sneak into my heart.

GRAYSON

Staring across the horizon of green fields, I notice that I don't have an aversion to all this family business talk. I thought I would be reluctantly listening all morning to my brothers explain crops, deliveries, and events scheduled.

Instead, I admire how great Olive Owl has become. Knox is the youngest of all of us but has worked hard from day one, ensuring we have the best produce around. He likes the rugged way of life, even if he doesn't look the part. Ask him which cow needs a vet or which week to plant pumpkins and he knows all the details.

Bennett is standing next to me with arms folded. "This is going to be a good year. We're all sold out for our weekend package in a few weeks." He works more on the business side and is always insistent on having events at Olive Owl. And I have to hand it to him, the romance packages and weekend wine tastings sell like hotcakes.

I notice Knox smirk as he drinks from his bottle of water. "Going to replay the last time you were here for a weekend event, Grayson?"

I roll my eyes as we begin to walk back toward the main house. "Okay, lay it on me. You haven't mentioned Brooke once today, and normally, ten minutes in you've mentioned her at least twice."

"Lucy shared the gossip that you finally had *the* run-in with Brooke," Bennett adds with flashing eyes.

"Yeah, Brooke and I said hello, and I met her the other night to catch up."

Bennett and Knox look at one another, as if they're debating who should speak.

"What?" I urge.

"Don't mess with her, okay?" Knox reminds me.

"Yeah, we like her more than you," Bennett adds, "and she's a good person who doesn't need her heart thrown around by you again. She's a mom now. She's helped us out with Lucy the past few years when Lucy needed a woman. There's more at stake." He opens the door to the main farmhouse that we had refurbished into a bed-and-breakfast with restaurant. I even designed the layout.

"I'm not going to be lectured by my younger brothers."

We each take a spot at the table in the middle of the restaurant. We aren't open for lunch every day, so we're alone.

"Bennett is right. You can't just waltz in here and slide into home base when you don't even consider this place home." Knox's tone has an edge, slight annoyance too.

"It's not that I don't consider this place home. I've just lived a different life," I clarify.

"Exactly. And unless you're sure you want a change, then don't mess around with her," Knox reaffirms his earlier point.

"Maybe you're being a little harsh, Knox. Those two deserve a chance." Bennett turns his attention to me. "What's the plan there? I mean, if you're back and she's here then maybe…" Bennett begins, and I feel like I should finish the sentence.

I've been thinking about it for days. I don't have an answer other than she has a rope tied to me and she has no clue. I'm not sure I can stay away. Her daughter isn't a deterrence either.

But I cop out on my answer. "No plan. Especially as she made it clear we should be neighbors only."

"Ouch." Bennett pats my back.

"Maybe a good policy," Knox says. "Anyhow, she comes here a lot with Rosie. I let them see the animals and we normally have a coffee."

"It's fine," I say. "Really, from my perspective, she can show up as many times as she wants." Because wearing her down may be an idea. What's the harm in a little flirtation to warm the waters?

"Morning, boys!" Helen's chirpy tone catches all our attention as she arrives at our table. The woman in her fifties has worked with us for years on a part-time basis, more helping with guests than anything.

We all greet her, and she gives me an extra-overdone smile. "And?"

My brothers both laugh before leaning back in their chairs for the show.

I give Helen an inquisitive look.

"When I was at the dentist this morning, Sally-Anne told me that Brooklyn is back from visiting her family. I assume that means…"

"Christ, you are as bad as my brothers. Can we change the topic?"

Helen looks disappointed. "It's a logical question, Grayson!"

I wave it off. "Relax. You're not missing any gossip."

"Fine, but you treat her right, Grayson. That woman is stronger than you think, and she deserves the best." Helen shimmies off.

I should be offended that everyone holds me in such low regard. However, I know what they're saying. Hell, I agree with them! And fuck it, I hate myself for the fact that a few of their points are true.

I'm the man who should have tried harder. Found a way to make distance work. Dragged her by the hand and found our way.

The drive back from Bluetop four years ago was the longest of my life because I knew the weekend with Brooke wasn't the closure we needed. Instead, it reopened a wound and then threw alcohol on it. For weeks, I debated calling her and asking her to visit. I didn't have an answer of how we would work, and even though I realized it didn't matter, I was too late.

She was pregnant with someone else's baby.

I'd never come back to Bluetop often before that whole episode, and I sure as hell came back even less after. I didn't really want to see her with someone else's kid.

But I should have been a better friend if anything, especially when I learned she was doing it all alone.

So yeah, everyone has their valid point.

"I'm here for the next few years with Brooke as my neighbor. How screwed am I?" I honestly ask my brothers.

"Depends," Bennett says as he rakes a hand through his hair. "If you really want to try then you have everything going for you; it could work."

Knox interrupts, "But if your plan is to get out of here as soon as Lucy graduates then you are royally screwed. You have two years of complete blue balls ahead of you."

Smiling to myself, I know neither of their outlooks are the

one for me. I will create my own path, take it one day at a time.

"Thanks," I reply simply. "Anyhow, how is Operation Driver's License?"

Bennett shakes his head then rubs a hand across his face. "It's awful. Lucy is a horrible driver."

I'm slightly confused. "She said you mentioned she could take her test soon."

"I don't have it in my heart to tell her she isn't a great driver. I already feel like some days she's going to put me in some ridiculous video on her social media."

Knox chuckles as he crosses his arms and leans back in the chair. "The last one went viral, man; I can understand the concern. But let's just aim that she has her license before summer. The independence will be good for her."

I have to remind us all of something. "Don't you recall what happened when we each got our license?"

Immediately, we all smile to ourselves.

"Fuuuuck." That isn't Bennett enjoying the memories. It's the sound of a frightened man.

Because I'm sure the summer he first got to drive solo was fueled with going to parties, late-night drive-thrus, and girls in the back of his car. I know this because that's what it was for me—except it was only one girl.

"Listen, either way, she will end up doing something we don't like. We have to accept that now," Knox says. He's unusually chill when it comes to Lucy, but that's just his personality.

"Speaking of Lucy, I should go pick her up from school." I glance at my phone for the time.

"Sure. Thanks for stopping by. Next time, I'll get you to work on checking the barrels," Knox warns me with a hint of humor.

"I'll leave that to you experts. But I will have the outlines for the new barn ready soon, and count me in for helping with the next wine-tasting event." I stand from my seat to head out.

"Wait! We found something when we were going through boxes of Dad's things." Knox's face lights up as he walks to the restaurant's bar and reaches over the counter to pull something up.

As he tosses me the jean jacket, I have to grin. "Wow, this is a throwback." I used to wear the thing all the time in high school and college. Thought it made me look cool. I traded it in for white dress shirts and blazers when I started working in the corporate world.

"We thought you could use it again since you may get a little dirtier here than your office. I hear you're even mowing the lawn these days," Bennett teases as he stands.

"You know, it's kind of weird having you back. It's like you never left." The honesty in Knox 's tone catches me off guard.

Because truthfully, even though I made another life for myself, it feels like I never left.

————

PULLING AWAY from the high school with a pissed-off Lucy in the passenger's seat is definitely my highlight of the day. I'm trying to keep calm, but when I saw Lucy talking to that little punk who had the eyes of a horny teenager, I lost it. I mean, I stayed in my car, but my scowl still hasn't faded.

Then when I told her that I changed my mind about the party, things went south.

"This isn't fair, you said I could go!"

"Life isn't always fair, Lucy."

"So basically, because you made a shit load of mistakes as a teenager, I have to live with the consequences of it."

Turning the corner, I sigh. "Kind of but no. Have Kendall come over, go to a movie, but let's avoid parties with seniors named Luke, who I guarantee will knock someone up by the time graduation hits, and let's not have that person be you."

"I can't believe this. It's bad enough I get stuck with the brother who was forced to move here but now he can't even be cool. You were always fun to hang out with before…"

I know what she means. She would visit me in Chicago all the time. I would let her drag me shopping, go to museums, check out cupcake hotspots. She only knew me as the brother who had a life away from Bluetop.

Now I'm a version of myself that I never would have predicted.

I sigh in agreement. "Before Dad passed? Yeah… Well, I'm sure he had some logical reasoning behind all of this."

"You know none of our lives have changed except yours. We've all been doing fine here. I'm sorry to uproot your spectacular life in the city." I hear the annoyance and hurt in her voice.

Abruptly, I pull the car to the side of the road and stare directly at her. "Lucy, don't say it like that! I'm here for you, not because he made me, and I don't regret that I'm back for you. Now, can we end this morbid conversation and decide what the hell we're eating for dinner?"

She studies me for a second before nodding.

Even though we have a minute of quiet as I make our way back to our house, I know she understands me.

By the time we get to our driveway, I'm quick to notice that Brooke is sitting outside on her porch watching Rosie play. I'm going to need to get used to seeing this scene.

"You need to make cookies," Lucy states.

I turn my head to her, confused.

"The booster club is having a bake sale. I'm supposed to bring cookies." She looks at me like I should know this.

Parking the car, I offer the obvious solution. "Okay, I'll pick some up at the store."

Lucy rolls her eyes and growls as she opens the car door. "No, we need to *bake* them, otherwise some of the moms get a little too judgmental."

I'm pretty sure I can march into the next parents meeting, flash a grin, and get the moms to agree to anything. I'm not above using the Blisswood charm to save me from baking. But I can't let Lucy know my tactics.

I groan as I close the car door behind me. "We'll find a how-to video or something."

"Ugh, this is going to go wrong," Lucy communicates her fear before throwing on a smile and waving to Rosie who's running toward her.

"Lucy, Lucy, Lucy!" Rosie yells.

Since Lucy has crossed the property line, I take it as my sign to follow. After all, need to rein in the kiddos, right?

Lucy quickly follows Rosie to her chalk on the driveway as Brooke slowly walks down the steps in my direction. Her hands find her back pockets and her hair is partly up. Her gentle smile makes me forget about the cookie dilemma.

"Hey," she greets me.

"Hey to you too."

"Rosie is crazy about Lucy, so this is probably going to happen a lot."

I plant a hand on my hip and offer her a smile. "Lucy doesn't seem to mind."

"A good day?"

I rub the stubble on my chin as my smile spreads. This is us making small talk apparently.

"Yeah, just at the farm, then a solid ten-minute debate with a sixteen-year-old. Just an average day."

"Everything okay?" Brooke glances over at Lucy then back at me.

"It's fine. She wasn't thrilled when I said she can't go to a party."

"Ouch," she whispers. "I'm surprised you made it out of the car."

"It's more like I saw her with some guy, and combine that with a party... yeah, been there, got the t-shirt."

Her tongue swirls inside her mouth, as if she can't control the beaming smile that wants to appear.

My eyes squint at her as I try to figure out what she's thinking. "What?" I ask.

"Just... just remembering you at her age. Parties, girls..."

"There wasn't girls. There was *a* girl. You were that girl... and I don't know, we were different." Because we were. Sure, Brooke and I made the appearance at every party thrown, but we would disappear just as quickly. We would go park somewhere and talk and make out, until we upgraded making out for other activities.

I never had any intention of hooking up with randoms at a party and that was that. No, we were Brooke and Grayson, junior and senior year. Social media was only just entering the scene, so it was easy to be in our own world. The couple everyone thought would marry and have three kids with a dog.

"I guess we were. I mean—" She can't finish, as Rosie comes squealing her way.

"Cookies, cookies, cookies!"

I look at Lucy, unamused she dropped the big C-word in front of a three-year-old.

"We should probably go sort that situation out," I note as I scratch the back of my head.

"This so isn't fair. I'm going to have to put in all the work because you have two left thumbs in the kitchen." Lucy crosses her arms in annoyance.

"Mommy!" Rosie pulls Brooke's shirt. "Can we make cookies?"

"Oh, uh—"

Lucy lights up at her suggestion. "Can I have your recipe? You make the best chocolate chip cookies."

My head tilts to the side. "Still making that recipe? Those were some *good* cookies." Mouthwatering and even better when she used to let me lick the spoon too.

Brooke smiles at everyone. "What is with all this cookie talk?"

"Apparently, there's the high school bake sale, and I will be crucified if I don't deliver home-baked goods," I explain and feel like a solution may be coming my way. I shrug a shoulder. "I mean, if it's to raise money for the wrestling team, then sorry, my efforts are not going to go far."

"It's for the baseball team so they can have new uniforms," Lucy chimes in.

I snap my fingers in the air. "Now that's a good cause. I guess we're going to be baking."

Brooke shakes her head and waves a hand. "Something tells me you are still horrible in the kitchen."

"My mommy makes the bestest cookies," Rosie proudly announces.

"I mean, I guess I could whip up a batch," Brooke offers and looks between us.

"Could you? Are you sure?" I throw in to double-check, but inside I'm celebrating.

"Brooke, you are so awesome. You're saving me too!" Lucy looks excited.

Brooke throws her hands up in the air as she shrugs her shoulders. "Sure, I can help."

"Great," I say. "I can go grab the ingredients from the store and we can get started."

Brooke turns all her attention to me, places her hands on her hips, and tilts her head at me. The way she used to when she was dismayed with me.

"*We* will bake away. *Ladies* only. I'm sure you don't really want to help anyhow." Before I can protest, her other hand tells me to stop. "My conditions or no cookies."

I give her a satisfied smirk. "Sure. But just remember I like a challenge."

Turning away to head to the store, I have to shake my head and smile to myself.

Because I would gladly have her throw a cookie or two my way.

5

BROOKE

This is not what I had in mind for today. I should grow a spine and learn how to stay rooted to the ground when Grayson is around. His suave grin will not fool me again.

But I look at Rosie, and she is so happy stirring another batch of dough, making a mess and squealing with Lucy. There are worse things I could be doing.

Glancing at the timer, I see our third batch is ready to be taken out of the oven. I lean over and open the oven with a towel in my hand to grab the tray.

"These smell so good." Lucy beams as she helps Rosie pour chocolate chips into a bowl.

"We just need to let them cool a bit. How many do you need for the bake sale?"

Lucy shrugs a shoulder. "I guess a few trays. I'm sure Grays will steal a few, so probably a little extra."

I nod at that thought as I begin to transfer cookies to the cooling rack with a spatula.

The doorbell confirms what I was waiting for. I know it'll be Grayson because he doesn't respond to rules.

"Last batch on the tray, ladies," I instruct as I head past them to the front door.

Opening the door, I'm already rolling my eyes and have a you-are-so-predictable look. "Grays." My tone is a bit more playful than I would like.

"Hey there, thought I should probably check in, possibly drag my sister away, steal a cookie. I mean, if you really need someone to taste test then I guess I can do it." He invites himself in, and his direct line for the kitchen feels like a throwback to the days when afternoons were snacks, home-work, and sex.

I exhale deeply as I move back to the crowd. Already Grayson has a spoon of dough, and Rosie looks kind of mad at him.

She points her little finger at him. "Mommy says we can't eat the dough."

Grayson's eyes look at me with a raised brow. "Oh dear, your mommy may need to put me in time-out."

"Eww." Lucy rolls her eyes.

I give Grayson an unimpressed look, but truthfully, I'm struggling not to smile.

"How is Operation Cookies going? Are we saved from the moms?" Grayson asks as he leans against the counter.

"I would think so," Lucy says. "Do you want me to take Rosie to wash her hands?" she offers, and looking at Rosie, I see she is a mess.

"Sure, I'll throw her in the bath later," I say.

My daughter's ears perk up. "Bath! Can we have bubbles?"

"Later, okay, kiddo? We still have cookies in the oven. Follow Lucy."

Watching the teenager lead my daughter off, I turn my

attention to Grayson who seems to have his eyes permanently glued on me.

"Thanks." His tone is soft and warm. "I really wouldn't be able to master cookie baking."

I shrug a shoulder. "I figured, and it's no problem. Rosie loved it."

"Hope it didn't set your day off too much."

I put my hands in the back pockets of my jeans as I go to lean against the counter next to him. "Nah, we take it easy in the afternoons."

"She's adorable, that's for sure."

Warmth spreads through me from his words or the pure thought that he and Rosie have met. Because I wish our timing had been different and that Grayson was here because we were his family. But I shake it off before I can think about it too deeply.

"So how much in the doghouse am I that I said Lucy can't go to the party? Did she talk about it?" he asks me.

A wry smile forms on my face. "I'm not divulging that intel, but don't be the guy who makes her sneak out."

His face turns slightly serious. "That bad, huh? It's her I trust, the guys not so much."

"If you trust her then what's the problem?"

"I don't know. I think it's more I'm trying not to think about my sister's romantic life, because then I don't need to address any bigger issues…" He adjusts his neck from the discomfort of the thought.

"You don't need to give her a sex talk if that's what you're worried about," I mention as I grab my now-cold mug of tea from the counter.

"I know I'm late to the game, I just don't think I can't *not* say anything. Wait a second, why are you so certain?" He angles his body to me as I realize I let something slip.

"Because... I talked with her one night when she was here to babysit." It was kind of awkward too because I couldn't exactly explain how my first experience went down, considering our dynamics.

Gray's mouth hitches up and an audible scoff escapes. "*You.* Okay, what did you say?"

"Nothing earth-shattering. It's not like I shared how my first time happened."

Our eyes catch and I know we're both thinking about it.

Grayson and I waited until I turned seventeen, not that a state law would have stopped us. It's Grays whose patience deserves a medal, as I wasn't his first. I doubt any Blisswood man made it past their sixteenth birthday a virgin. He knew what he was waiting for.

His dad was away at a conference, and his brothers, I don't know, seemed to know to give us space. I never did ask if he made them swear to some code. His house was quiet, and it was raining out. Then, there in his bed, we became one. He was so worried about hurting me, so tentative and slow. It was beautiful, down to the candles he had lit. For weeks we had been anticipating it, and when I came over that night, we just knew it was our night.

It was just as perfect as our last time together.

"Wow, we are heading back to the early days." He smirks to himself. "Look, thanks for letting Lucy bug you. She doesn't really have an adult female in her life."

"Well, I am kind of the poster child for unexpected pregnancy. I think she gets the memo to be careful." I gesture to myself and nervously joke.

"You're also an adult with a decent job. You have a lot more going for you."

It's comforting that our conversation moves with ease,

despite the years that have passed. His eyes have this way of making me feel special.

Our heads turn to the sound of Lucy and Rosie coming back.

"Mommy, when is Lucy babysitting again?" my daughter asks as she sneakily reaches for a cookie.

Pushing the tray away, I lift my daughter up in my arms. "Well, I need to ask her, but I was hoping soon."

"Since I am confined to my habitat by my brother then I have a free weekend schedule." Lucy throws on the dramatics which only makes me snort a laugh.

"Hey, I was considering letting you go to the party, but with an attitude like that, I might change my mind again," Grayson announces as he flashes me a wink before we both watch Lucy's face immediately change.

"Really?" Excitement fills her voice, and he nods in agreement. "Yes! Kendall will be so happy she doesn't have to go alone."

"Sounds like you're too busy to babysit," I note.

"Not Friday. Friday I'm free," Lucy confirms.

Perfect timing, actually. "Oh, well, if you want to babysit then I can go to the bar with Kelsey," I coo with my daughter in my arms.

"Ah, Fridays at Rooster Sin. Predictable." Lucy's tone feels like she is the wizard of knowledge, and it's humorous.

"That's funny, because I am sure my brothers mentioned I should check out two-for-one on beers. I guess I will see you there," Grayson gloats before popping a cookie into his mouth.

"Shouldn't you be her designated driver?" Lucy suggests to her brother.

"Uhm, I think I'm good," I interrupt. "I don't really drink much, if at all."

Grayson leans against the kitchen cupboard casually. "I don't know, B. I should be setting an example for the young one." His tone is pure trouble as he indicates with his head to Lucy. "Let me be the designated driver for the night. You don't have to worry about driving."

Walking to the other side of the kitchen, I say, "Really, I've been fine the last four years, so I'm sure I can handle another night without your assistance."

"Mommy, he has a shiny car," my daughter states her thoughts as she plays with the fabric of my sweater.

"Don't be ridiculous. We're heading to the same destination," he tries to persuade me.

"Maybe you'll want to leave at a different time, so it wouldn't work," I try to justify as I reach for the Tupperware.

"I mean, unless you have other plans then I'm good. Happy to work around your schedule." His eyes never blink as his cheeky look remains fixed.

"It's better this way," Lucy says to me. "Last time you went to Rooster Sin, you were rocking those skinny jeans you have. I mean, guys must have gone crazy."

I did look hot that one time, with black skinny jeans that fit me like a glove.

Grayson's eyes go wide. "Now I'm definitely picking you up and we can drive together."

"Cool," Lucy says before I can speak. "Text me what time you want me to come over on Friday. We'll take the cookies and get out of your hair. A lifesaver, as always. Thanks, Brooke. Make sure my brothers buy you a drink or two Friday." Lucy quickly throws cookies into the Tupperware box.

It's a blur what happens the next few minutes until I'm alone with Rosie and realize that Hurricane Grayson just came through, and I suddenly feel like I am going on a date this Friday.

It's the opposite of what I should want in this moment.

What's worse is that nobody comes out of a Friday at Rooster Sin unscathed...

———

THE SOUNDS of Walker Hayes play on the radio as I sit on the front seat in Grayson's car. The smell of leather is slightly overpowering, as he keeps his SUV clean. We've been quiet the last two minutes.

It was easy to be distracted when Lucy arrived, and I got her settled with Rosie and a box of mac 'n cheese. Then I went out to the driveway to find Grayson leaning against the front of his car waiting for me.

Admittedly, his scorching look is way better than what my mind has been imagining the past few days as I prepared for tonight. He's even rocking the jean jacket he had back in the day; he must have done that on purpose to get a rise out of me. I used to love when he would take it off and drape it over my shoulders to keep me warm, because I was *his girl*.

As I wrap hair around my finger, I remind myself that this isn't a date. Kelsey will be there, Knox and Bennett too. It's a usual Friday night at the local bar. Nothing special.

My sweater dress with ankle boots is just the ticket to feel cute and comfortable.

"Temperature okay?" he asks as he focuses on the road.

In the car, yes. My body, not exactly.

"It's fine."

"So, do you go to Rooster Sin often?"

"Not a lot, maybe once a month. I can't be on mom duty

twenty-four seven." It's important for me to have a night off, and I don't need to feel guilty about that.

He side-glances to me. "That's good, B, you deserve a break. And since you're off mom duty, then tell me something non-child-related."

I grin at this request. "Not much to say. Bluetop is the same as it's always been. The band tonight is pretty good. Or at least improved from a few months ago since rumor has it that they actually practice now. Everyone still gossips like crazy, and I'm sure Sharon Clark will latch onto you like the old days."

In high school she didn't care who was in a relationship or not. She went for guys like a vulture in heat. Now in our twenties, she's no different.

"I'm positive she and Bennett hooked up at one point," he mentions, and I am not surprised.

"Probably. But it's nice that all the Blisswood guys show up, considering your vineyard is kind of competition."

Grayson's low laugh sounds almost humorously evil. "Not even close. Olive Owl is an establishment with high standards and wine. Rooster Sin has peanut shells on the floor and cheap alcohol."

"True." It's no secret that the Blisswood family has done well financially.

We pull into the parking lot, with the neon sign blinking up high and people heading into the bar. The sound of music and people chatting already hits us and we're not even out of the car yet.

"I would open the door for you, but considering you gave me death eyes when I helped you into the car earlier, lesson learned."

Hopping out of the car, I stand on SUV's running board

and point my gaze to him over the roof of the car. "Yep. Not a date, just neighbors carpooling," I proudly state my opinion.

When he hits the lock button on the fob of his car, his pointed look sends excitement through my body.

"Sure, sweetheart, whatever you want to tell yourself."

Heading to the door, I'm not blind to the fact that he's walking next to me, or that his hand casually falls to my lower back as he opens the door for me. A gentleman he is, but with me, it feels more like territorial claim, and my nipples respond to that fact.

Entering the bar and the room is happening. A man whistles as the band retunes between sets, and there's a solid line of people sitting at the bar.

"What are you drinking?" Grayson offers by leaning to my ear, his breath hitting my skin with warm heat.

"Oh, uhm, just a beer is fine."

He steps back and I swear his eyes glimmer at me. "Sounds good. Want to sit somewhere?"

"I think Kelsey or your brothers saved a table." I begin to scan the room, and halfway through my search, I have a strange feeling that I should be pissed off, yet I am somehow excited.

There is not one best friend or Blisswood brother in sight.

Pulling my phone out of my bag, I see a text from Kelsey.

KELSEY

> Sorry. Forgot I need to do the laundry. I'm sure you'll have fun.

A laughing emoji accompanies the message. I quickly respond.

> Me: Wow! We will be having words.

Grayson nudges my arm and offers me a bottle of beer.

"Find them?"

Gulping my drink, I hide any nerves I may have. "No, uhm, Kelsey had to cancel. Your brothers, where are they?" Stupid question, as I know the answer.

He steps around me with a sly yet so ridiculously smooth grin. "They may have had a change of plans."

"Right."

"Come on, there's a quiet booth in the corner."

"Let me guess, you had that planned too?" I give him an inquisitive look as I bite my inner cheek.

"Nah, that's just fate giving us a hand. Now come on, let's have a good night," he urges, and without hesitation, I follow to our small intimate table in the corner where he chooses to slide next to me when he could easily sit across from me.

With our arms brushing as he sits close, he glances to his side to plant his sight on me.

"Time to be honest with me," he says. "Something I've been wondering about."

"What's that?"

"The truth about Rosie."

Immediately, my heart sinks.

GRAYSON

I t's taking all my power not to crash my lips onto Brooke's mouth, covered in pink Chapstick that I bet tastes like watermelon. The slight catch of her breath and her eyes having a hint of fear tells me she's afraid of what direction I'm going to take our conversation.

"What about Rosie?" A wave of protectiveness fills her voice.

I can only offer her a reassuring smile as I nudge her arm with my own. "I mean, if Rosie wasn't in the picture, would you still be this reluctant around me? I get it, I do. But I can't help but wonder."

A look that can only be described as relief spreads across her face, and I really hope I manage to touch her by the end of the night.

"Grays," she begins, and I can see she's debating what to say. "I think last time around is your answer. We didn't even last an hour before we ended up naked."

"Good times," I acknowledge before I take a swig of my beer from the bottle.

I love it when she blushes, and her head turning slightly

to the side makes me want to fucking dive into the spot on her neck that is begging me to nip and suck.

"I don't really want to talk about it, Grayson. The fact is you are only back because your father put it in his will; otherwise, you have no reason to be here."

I struggle to answer, because to everyone, that's what it would seem. But I am back, and reminders of what I've walked away from are overbearing and inescapable. Seeing Brooke again makes me remember that I always thought *what if*. What if I asked her to move to the city, what if I reached out more, what if I was an actual man who fought for what he wanted.

But alas, at eighteen I was an idiot, and four years ago I was blinded by my career. And even though I debated how to make it work until the moment she crushed me with her news, I don't want to sound like a selfish asshole who didn't know how to navigate your ex being pregnant with someone else's kid.

"Maybe it's good that I'm back," I admit aloud for the first time.

Her head perks up in surprise as she focuses her attention on me. "How so?"

"I don't know. The slower pace of life is kind of refreshing. It's actually relaxing. Not the roping-in-a-teenager part, but the routine, you know? Make sure Lucy actually shows up to class, draw my designs while working from home, lunch with my brothers on a regular basis. Don't get me wrong, I miss how anything and everything can be delivered in ten minutes when you live in the city or the options of what you can do on the weekend. Staying in fancy hotels and traveling business class kind of loses the wow factor after a while. I guess the hustle is missing from Bluetop," I reflect as I lean back casually.

"It's not like we're in the complete boonies," she teases me, because she is a proud Bluetop citizen—never tried to leave, and I don't think she ever wants to. "I mean, I still manage to make it to a Target without needing to road trip it. Plus, the coffee in town has gotten better since this hip couple from Portland moved here. And not to mention, Sally-Anne even won the best pie in the state last year."

"Is that why there was a line a mile long outside her bakery last Saturday? I wanted to pick up some cinnamon rolls, but that plan went out the window when I saw the waiting time."

"Oh, that's a shame you missed out."

Damn, I love the way her lips wrap around the bottle.

I have to grin. "Nah, she saw me, and I flashed my smile then she let me skip the line."

Brooke's cute and bubbly laugh erupts. "It's no joke, that Blisswood charm. Your father was the same way. He would always pick up muffins for me since taking Rosie to a bakery is like walking through a minefield."

I scratch my chin as I stiffen slightly from the mention of my father.

She picks up on it. "You never really… I don't know… Are you at peace with how the last year went?"

"I did visit him in the hospital. Maybe not like Bennett or Knox did. I would normally drive up and back the same day. Quick visits, and yeah, we were okay in the end. He even stayed with me in Chicago a few times when he had treatments. But we were never not okay, you know? We were just neutral," I explain, and her hand reaches out to squeeze my arm for comfort, and it's the best comfort I've had in recent months.

"I know. And you seem okay, actually. Maybe even calmer than a few years ago." Her eyes linger over me, and I wonder if she feels just as warm as I do in this moment. The understanding between us is still strong, we don't need a lot of words.

Our eyes hold, and I wonder what would happen if I touched her hand. Like she's mine. It would be even better if I were to take her out of here and give her a bruising kiss to remind her that whether we like it or not, no matter if factors align, we will end up in each other's arms. We don't need to know anything else when it comes to one another.

Before I have a chance to interlace our fingers, a deep voice interrupts us. "Grays! Grayson Blisswood, the legend returns."

Looking up, I see Coach Dingle. He appears the same as he did when I was on the varsity baseball team. Old, a donut too many, and the image of a good man who goes to Sunday church and invites the whole team over for dinner.

"Coach Dingle," I say as I stand to shake his hand.

"I heard you were back, and I was hoping to run into you. I would love for you to stop by the field." He slaps a hand on my shoulder.

I laugh at the mere suggestion. "It's been a while since I played. Not sure you want me on your field." Sure, I go for a run a few times a week and lift some weights, but I'm not benching anything spectacular.

"Nonsense. I'm sure you still have that arm in ya. And those boys don't need someone to show them the ropes, they have the skill already."

"Still hoping to make state?" I give him a raised brow.

He waves a hand at me. "Boy, we will. No, they need someone as a role model, to listen to. We have some good boys on the team, but they lack a little direction. Missing someone in their life to give them a hand."

"Again, me?"

He squeezes my shoulder. "Yeah, you, Mr. Big Shot. I'm sure you have a lot to offer."

"I'll think about it," I say.

Dingle grins and shakes my hand before bidding me farewell and wishing Brooke a good evening.

As I slide back into the booth, Brooke is trying not to giggle. "You are still the town's golden boy."

I shake my head at her opinion. "If only they knew. I'm the guy who has no problem firing someone and can get a little demanding."

"Oh, I know." The way she playfully says that as her eyes go bold and she drinks from her beer makes me intrigued.

"Care to elaborate?"

She quirks her mouth as she chooses her words wisely. "You've definitely changed in some departments."

Moving closer to her, I rest my arm behind her on the back of the booth. "In bed, you mean?"

"Something like that."

In my head, I remember a few years ago with her. Pinning her to the bed with one hand and sliding her dress up with the other. That was before I made her beg for me and flipped her to her stomach. And that was only round one. It's true, I like it one way in the bedroom department—with me in charge.

This night feels like it's looking up for me. Conversation runs easily, and I think she is enjoying the night despite her initial hesitation.

"Want another drink?" I offer, and to my surprise, she doesn't debate and nods in agreement.

Quickly, I make my way to the bar and order another round. Rooster Sin is always fast, and I get our drinks quickly. When I return to the table, I notice Brooke swiping on her phone, the weather app.

"Here you are." I slide the beer to her.

"Thanks. Just checking the weather. There's a front coming through later tonight so I want to make sure I'm home for Rosie. She hates storms."

"Most kids do, right?"

"That they do." She offers me her bottle to clink in cheers, a sort of peace offering.

"To neighbors." I crack a smirk.

"Neighbors." Her eyes study me, and it feels like nobody's in the place but us. "So, did you have this planned all week?"

"No, really, I meant it when I said fate. Literally, Bennett called me as I was waiting in your driveway."

She squints one eye at me. "Hmm, I may investigate that story."

I hold my hands up in surrender. "By all means, do."

"OH. MY. GOODNESS." Holy fuck, the obnoxious voice of Sharon Clark hasn't changed.

Brooke and I glance up to the blonde-haired woman with a dress too small who is towering over us.

"Well, isn't this a throwback. Grayson and Brooke two-point-oh." The gum she chews only adds to her squeaky voice.

From instinct, I wrap an arm around Brooke's shoulder to pull her closer to me.

"Good to see you," are the only polite words that I can think of.

"You two are, like, together again?"

"Catching up," Brooke corrects her with a mundane tone.

Sharon casts her gaze on me as if she's assessing a prize. "Oh, so Grays, you're on the market?"

I can feel Brooke cringe in my hold. I'm going to guess it's from Sharon's choice of words.

"You know, something tells me I am probably going to be

busy with this one here." I indicate to Brooke and offer Sharon a wink.

Sharon lets a sound of discontent escape. "Well, call me if you want to have a fun night sometime." She wiggles her fingers in the air before heading off to some friends.

Brooke clears her throat, and I have to glance at her with an amused look. "Okay there?"

"Sure. You should take her up on her offer." Her eyes try to avoid me.

"Never going to happen. Plus, there's someone else I want to make me an offer." I wait for her to shoot her gaze my way.

The moment she does, I feel like I have her.

"Not happening. Our adult selves had our fun four years ago."

I notice that I haven't moved my arm from her, nor has she jerked it away.

"Wow, you really are going to keep me at bay."

"I'm not the same person, Grays."

I hate how she says it like it would be a disappointment to me, when it's the exact opposite. "You're still independent and stubborn, that hasn't changed."

She straightens her posture and shakes off my arm. "Everyone thinks I'm sweet, but with you, I don't know how to be."

"I'm listening." I let my finger glide along her arm because I need to touch her.

"With you I only know how to be honest. I'm not fragile to you or the sweet Brooklyn that everyone feels sorry for because she's a single mom."

Christ, I hate that she even thinks like that.

I'm not going to have it. I don't care, and I take her hand in mine. "You have it all wrong. You are strong and raising a great kid. And you are still sweet to me."

She looks at me, curious.

Leaning in, I brush her hair to the side so I can whisper next to the shell of her ear. I inhale her scent of berries and turn on my raspy voice. "I remember how you taste and that is perfectly sweet."

I need to taunt her to make her smile, and I do so with honesty. So what if it's yet again a reminder of what we both can't forget.

The slow smile forming on her mouth tells me she isn't mad at my truth.

"You're still trouble, Grayson Blisswood," she softly purrs before letting our foreheads touch because that is her way of teasing me. By letting me within breathing distance of her mouth that I could easily touch with my own.

But I respect her too much right now.

"Can we go get some fresh air?" she asks.

"Good idea." Because this is the last place I want to be. In public, as I'm being slowly tortured for all to see.

———

THE COOL SPRING air is exactly what we need.

Walking to the car, we say nothing but allow our bodies to brush along one another's sides.

When we get into my car, I debate if I should try my luck and ask if she wants to drive somewhere or go to the drive-thru and order a milkshake and fries. Something we used to do. I bet she still loves to do it.

"A little drive-thru?"

"Actually, that sounds—" Lightning brightening the sky causes her to stop her sentence, and instead, her look turns concerned. "Sounds good, but could we head home? I don't want Lucy to have to deal with Rosie with the storm coming."

No hesitation. "Absolutely. I'll get us home in ten." Instead of the usual fifteen.

Brooke's hand reaches over to touch mine on top of the middle console. She gives me a look of appreciation.

The rest of the ride home, Brooke is nervous. I don't dare joke with her or try and make small talk, as she continues to look at the sky and her phone app. Fair enough, spring storms in the Midwest can turn quickly.

And as I pull us up to our houses and we get out of the car, we get our answer to what kind of storm this is going to be as the tornado siren goes off. It's not unusual for these parts but completely unpredictable if it's a false alarm or not.

"Come on, let's grab the girls and head downstairs." I quickly place my hand on Brooke's back to guide her inside.

Already, I know this night is long from over.

7

BROOKE

Opening the door to the house, I immediately hear my daughter crying and see Lucy bouncing Rosie in her arms. My hands instinctively reach out to take her, and I notice that for once Lucy's also slightly scared.

"She woke up when the thunder started," Lucy says nervously as she looks at her brother.

"I thought so," I say. "Come on, let's go downstairs." I kiss my daughter's forehead.

We all make our way to the basement, and I'm thankful that my parents refurbished the place a few years ago, so there's carpet and a sofa. I just never go down here because basements freak me out when alone.

Lucy sits on the floor cross-legged and starts to swipe on her phone. I go to sit on the couch.

"Jelly," Rosie cries as she clings to me, and tears fall. Glancing down, I realize we're missing the unicorn.

I silently curse to myself, and Grayson notices. "The unicorn," I explain.

"I'll go. Where is it?" He's already halfway back to the stairs.

"Her bedroom, I think. Are you sure?"

He flashes me a look that tells me he's got this, before disappearing like Superman.

"Kendall says the wind is picking up at her house," Lucy announces, glancing up from her screen.

"It'll be okay. We have these all the time."

I continue to stroke my daughter's hair and can imagine how the siren scares her.

"Got her!" Grayson returns, jiggling the unicorn in the air. He comes to sit next to us and hands the unicorn to Rosie who instantly grabs hold of the stuffed toy, and her eyes stay fixed on Grayson.

My nerves skyrocket from the mixture of the storm and the appeal that my daughter seems to have instantly taken to Grayson.

"You okay there, kiddo? It'll be over before you know it," he assures her and pats the unicorn's head.

"They say a tornado touched down five miles from here." Lucy wiggles her phone in the air.

Grayson waves for her to join us on the couch, and since Lucy has let down the independent-fearless-teenager persona, she quickly moves to sit next to him, causing all of us to squish together.

"We are safe and sound here. We'll just wait it out," he assures us all, as one arm goes to side-hug his sister and the other he uses to pull me close to him.

Our eyes meet and I'm thankful he's here.

"Hope this passes soon," I mention. "Last year, we had one night when the siren went off three times." I look to see that Rosie is poking Grayson with her stuffed toy.

"It is the season, but they normally miss us." He focuses his attention on Rosie. "Why is her name Jelly?"

"She's purple like grape jelly," Rosie answers.

He smiles at her answer. "Makes sense. You know your mom used to love peanut butter and jelly sandwiches and only with grape jelly."

"She still does." Rosie's pitch begins to diminish which tells me that she is slightly less hysterical as she hiccups a few tears.

"And how old is Jelly?" He continues to focus his attention on her.

"Uhm." She holds up one finger to indicate the number one.

"A baby unicorn then. Does Jelly go everywhere with you?"

She nods her head yes.

"Rosie loves unicorns and horses. We go to Olive Owl to see Lucy's horsey, don't we?" I remind her, and I feel her easing.

"Do you think the animals are okay?" Lucy asks her brother in a hushed tone.

He glances at her. "Knox and Bennett have it covered. This isn't new."

"Mommy." My daughter's sing-songy tone has returned. "Are we going to stay down here all night?

"I don't know, kiddo, probably just a bit longer."

The sound of the wind picking up mixes with the siren, and Grayson and I both look at one another, concerned. We both pull the girls closer.

He mouths to me *it's okay,* and I allow myself to scoot closer to him so he can keep a protective arm around us.

We sit there for a few minutes more until the wind lessens and the siren stops.

Grayson nudges his sister. "Lucy, can you check your

phone to see what they're saying—the weather service, *not* what Kendall is saying—I can't reach my phone." Because Grayson has a pile of humans clinging to him for safety.

Lucy swipes and types like crazy. "Looks like it's going to be awhile. We're on a tornado watch until three in the morning. Seems like more storms are on the way." She displays her phone so we can look at the radar.

"Let me go check upstairs." He untangles from us and heads to the stairs.

"Be careful," I call out. Looking to Lucy, I ask her, "Alright?"

She nods her head. "Sure. Rosie was asleep until right before you got home, I swear."

"Don't worry about it. I figured she would wake so we came back early."

Lucy's eyebrows raise. "Oh, so it wasn't because you were having a bad time?"

I can't help but smile at her matchmaking tendency. "Lucy, your brother and I are friends, okay?"

"But you weren't always that way. The girlfriends he's had the last few years were all awful, like not even smart or compatible. With you, he's… Grays, the good Grays. The version we all like. He looks at you differently than the others," she offers her view, and I debate how to process it. I know he hasn't always been single, but also know there was never anyone serious. The fact that I'm the one who seems to have a special effect on him makes me beyond happy. Probably more than it should.

Grayson interrupts us by arriving at the bottom of the stairs. "The storm seems to be moving to the east. Should be okay for now, but more storms are coming."

"Ugh, I'm tired and want to sleep but can't." Lucy sulks as she stands and moves to the stairs.

I stand and walk with Rosie in my arms. "I guess I should double-check if I even have a flashlight in case the power goes off."

"Let me do that. How about Lucy and I stay for a little longer?" he offers, and immediately I wonder what he means by stay.

I can't help but chortle at the suggestion but realize he's serious.

I ignore his suggestion and hand him Rosie without thought. "Here. Can you take Rosie for a second? It's easier to look myself than explaining where I probably have the flashlight."

While they head to the living room, I quickly run to the laundry room between the kitchen and garage, scavenging in a box for the flashlight until I find it. Returning to the living room, I see that Lucy is getting comfortable on the sofa with a blanket.

My eyes dart down the hall to Rosie in Grayson's arms as she leans her head against his chest. Her eyes are in a drowsy daze as he tucks Jelly securely between her and his chest.

The melting inside me isn't from the cuteness of the scene, although it's pretty damn sweet. No, it's the scene of a wish, of two people connecting and the speck of doubt within me, refusing to believe that it could be more.

The two people who have played the greatest role in my life, together in an embrace in front of me.

My heart feels full, right, but I'm not ready for any possibilities for this to be more.

———

GRAYSON slowly and gently lays Rosie in her bed, careful not to wake her. Quickly, I splay a blanket across her and admire that she fell asleep so easily.

Stepping away, we both appreciate the innocence of Rosie sleeping. In another dream, this would have been us on a daily occurrence.

We step into the hallway, and I debate if I should offer a cup of tea. There is no way I can sleep, especially as I hear thunder in the distance again so know this moment of silence will be temporary.

"She likes you," I say. "Otherwise, we would still have her screaming right now. You're good with her too."

"Oh yeah?" His half-smile is laced with pride as he leans against the wall and crosses his arms. "Don't really have experience with kids. You okay? I remember how much you hate nights like this."

I step closer to him and know this is a move of no return. "I'm okay. It's kind of nice having people here. We haven't had any tornados this year yet, but during storms, I normally bring Rosie into my bed, and we cuddle all night."

"Bet she loves that."

His hand touches my arm, inviting me to step into his embrace. I walk into his arms willingly because it feels like safety, affection, and a return to home.

The clap of thunder is the only sound as our eyes meet for recognition, asking one another if we're ready for it. The moment we both can't deny we want and need in this second.

His fingers trace the outline of my jaw before grazing my cheek, and it causes me to take more by nuzzling against his hand. I remind myself to breathe, as I feel the sensitive wave riding through me and it's making me light. But his hand glides through my hair before landing at the back of my neck to hold me firmly. He's got me, he will root me down.

The feeling of Grayson's other arm encircling my waist as he pulls me flush to his body is a firm reminder of how well we fit together. I can't help but press into his body as my eyes travel down from his eyes to his mouth.

"Grays—" My whispered plea is stopped by his lips touching mine, slowly at first.

I don't move and instead wait for his mouth to mold firmly against mine. The feeling of his soft lips mixed with stubble is a gentle reminder that he's grown into a man. His tongue slips into my mouth, seeking out my own, and I give it to him.

Entwining our tongues, I murmur into his mouth as my arms wrap around his neck. I angle my head so he can take more from me. If I'm already making a mistake, might as well make it a good one.

His hand tangles in my hair to hold me in place, a pure turn-on. He knows how he likes it as he nips the corner of my mouth while we catch a breath, before he devours my mouth and swallows my breath and murmur of approval.

How can a man's kiss be so demanding yet affectionately sweet?

As much as I want to take more from him, I need to breathe, and I reluctantly pull away with a gasp as his thumb traces my swollen bottom lip.

"This… this…" I'm unable to form a sentence as I glance around the scene.

I know Rosie is asleep and Lucy is too, both out of view. But this isn't the time for a reunion for our mouths.

"Don't overthink this, B," he whispers before kissing my forehead tenderly.

Gently pushing him away by using my fingertips pressed against his chest, I stay in his arms but create some distance.

"This can't happen," I remind him.

"It already has." His eyes pierce me, and I know I'm already heading down a path of no return as I untangle from his arms, just as the sound of thunder comes closer.

8

GRAYSON

Dragging the branch to the side of the yard, I replay the events of last night in my head.

After round two to the basement when another line of storms came through, I went home with Lucy. We were all exhausted, and I wasn't in the mood for Brooke to insist we shouldn't get closer, although her body made it clear that she wants the opposite.

Kissing her again lit a fire inside of me. I want to hold her more, kiss her more, and hell, my hands and dick have a few plans too.

I watch as Brooke drives up her driveway on this cloudy Saturday. I know this is our awkward next-day conversation coming our way.

Pressing my foot down onto the branch, I continue on my quest to clear the yard from debris after the storm. All the while, my eyes can't part from her every move as she gets out of the car and stares at me.

"Hey," she gently greets me as she places a few strands of hair behind her ear. "What are you doing?"

"I thought I could clear the yard for you."

"Oh."

"Neighbors," I clarify as I throw another branch to the pile. "Where's Rosie?"

"She has a birthday party for a friend. Lucy?"

"Olive Owl."

Our simple conversation is a cover for the fact that each of us is probably screaming a thousand thoughts inside.

"Look, you don't need to help. It's a nice gesture but..." She swallows as if she's unsure around me.

Pulling the garden gloves off, I make a mental note that it's been a good while since I've had Timberlands, jeans, and a t-shirt on to resemble a man who is one with wilderness.

"Going to do this again? Pull away?" I give her a knowing glare as I step in her direction.

She shakes her head, slightly irritated. "It's better this way, trust me."

I continue my journey closer to her, causing her to step back. "Why? What is it that has you so hesitant when I'm involved?"

She scoffs a bitter laugh. "You are a smart man, Grayson, you know the answer."

"No, I don't." I want to find out. Unravel her until she's lying under me and I'm inside of her.

"I have a daughter to think about, Grays, and quite frankly, I'm not in the mood for you to hurt me again." She turns to head into the garage, and I follow, as I'm on a mission.

The instant we step under the roof of the garage, I grab her arm. "What the hell does that mean?"

"I won't be that woman who just lets you waltz in when all you want is to leave. I'm never going to be enough for you." She jerks her arm out of my hold and storms off, but I stalk after her with an equal sharpness to my mood.

"Why do you think that?"

Brooke turns again, and I notice her chest moving up and down. "You want to know why?"

"Yes!"

"Because I was never part of your plans or dreams. Not at eighteen when you went to college and not four years ago when you had that fancy promotion. I was never going to be the reason you came back to Bluetop. Hell, you've been avoiding me for four years, every time you snuck into town. Message received."

Immediately I grab both of her arms with urgency and my blood boils from anger because she has it all wrong. I can't let her think this way.

"You're right, I fucked up. I owe you a big apology, because in my head, my career was everything. I owe you an even bigger fucking apology because I could have asked how you were, how it is being a mom, a million questions to make sure you were alright, but I never did." I feel my breath strain from the hurt in my tone.

"I'm not even mad at you for that. Because given the circumstances and our history, it kind of made sense. No, what I am furious about is because I feel like an awful person, because I can't help thinking that you came back for your sister but not me. There is a simple answer for that... I'm not enough."

Shaking my head, I tighten my grip on her arms. "You have it so fucking wrong. Because after last time together, I couldn't focus for days. I debated every scenario in the book of how we could make a relationship work. I hated waking up and not having you there. I swear, if you hadn't called me, I was about to get in my car and drive here to convince you to try." I lay it all out as our eyes remain in a tense gaze.

"Well, then... joke's on us. Timing had other plans," she

says softly, and I hate the sadness in her tone and the frown on her face.

"But here we are now, B. I'm here." I move my hands to cup her face to soothe her, her eyes misty. Does she not see the possibility?

In this moment, I realize, through her vulnerability that she has laid on the line, that she needs a reminder that she is worthy.

"For how long, though," she states simply.

She needs reassurance. She needs a man who won't let her down. All week, I've wondered what my plan was to cope with her living next to me. It's so simple. I want her, and I can't screw it up this time. I need to do better by her, and I'm going to have to show her. It's going to take fucking patience too.

"I need you to stop thinking for one minute and tell me what you feel between us right now." I stroke her cheeks with my thumbs as her hands hold my wrists.

"Don't do this, please," she begs in a whisper.

I kiss her cheek, then the corner of mouth before nudging her nose with mine. Coaxing her to ease into me, to this, whatever is about to transpire between us.

"Tell me to stop," I dare her in a low voice as my mouth trails along her jawline.

Her hands grab the fabric of my shirt, and she grips on at my chest. "I can't," she rasps right before my mouth crashes down onto hers.

My arms wrap around her shoulders to pull her to me because I have no plan to let her go. Our kiss turns frantic as we kiss again and again, our hands roaming because we don't know where to begin.

Without parting, I walk her backward to the door of the house, and we make it through as one before I have her pinned against the hallway wall. I kiss her deeper, greedily, her murmurs evaporating into my mouth as I devour her.

My hand moves down her body with haste to trace the shape of her ass, encouraging her to bring her legs up. They wrap around me as her arms enclose around my neck. I take all I can get and kiss her neck, making a trail to her collarbone as her head falls back.

I can't get enough of her watermelon smell. Or the softness of skin. Don't even get me started on her little whimpers when my tongue darts out to tease her skin.

Our lips meet again, and she mumbles from the back of her throat.

I should take my time with Brooke, show her how special she is, cherish every inch of her, but that's going to have to be for later. There is no way I'm taking our demanding urge right now down a notch.

This is all go until we both reach the release we both crave.

Reluctantly parting our lips, I step back, and she helps me yank my shirt off. My eyes watch her measure me up and her heavy breathing seems to show her approval. I slide down her body until I am on my knees before her. Her fingers entwine in my hair, encouraging me to keep going.

I pull at the button of her jeans and work on peeling the fabric down. My eyes peer up to watch her toy with me and slowly tantalize me by taking the edge of her shirt and sliding the fabric up to give me a peek of what's underneath— fucking lace.

With her jeans off, I notice she's wearing matching charcoal-gray lace, and when she tilts her hips to me, I get a glimpse that it's a thong, and her ass looks firm. Fuck!

I'm lost for which choice to make, where to start. I want

to do it all to her. But with her body already writhing before me, I don't want my girl to wait.

I kiss up her silky-smooth legs as I work my way back up. I stop between her legs to lick her over the lace, feeling her heat and dampness against my tongue. Teasing her over the fabric, I can already taste her sweetness seeping through. I can't help it and I need a taste; I slide the fabric to the side to lap up her juices and hit her clit.

Her moan makes my cock harder; she's wet and ready.

One more lick and I quickly get back to standing, my fingers gripping her jaw to force her gaze on me.

"Still as sweet as I remember."

Brooke's eyes hood closed at my words, and her hands reach for my belt, pulling me closer to her.

"Tell me you want this, B," I remind her that I'm still waiting for her words, but I know it's coming, so I take over, losing the belt and my pants.

"I…" Her breath is ragged. "I… Give it to me, Grayson. Don't make us think right now."

I nod gently to her in understanding as I step out of my pants. Her hand instantly seeks out my cock to cup, and she lowers my boxer briefs, causing my cock to spring to full attention. Her hand stroking me and my own groan causes me to lean forward and rest into her neck, enjoying her hands on me.

"Can I take you like this?" I tenderly kiss her neck as I seek permission.

"Yeah. IUD."

With that confirmation, I grab her hands and guide them above her head. Both of my hands pin her wrists to the wall as our bodies grind against one another, causing friction.

I readjust so my left hand holds her wrists above her head

and my other hand guides my cock to align with her, sliding in a few inches, her gasp telling me to go slow.

But then she fights my hold and breaks her hands free to plant on my hips, urging me to go deep and do it now. She's still half-dressed and it's fucking hot, evidence that we couldn't wait.

I move and her pussy envelopes around my cock, and it feels like nirvana. With abruptness, I thrust into her as her hands travel up my back, her nails digging into my skin, her leg coming up to my waist, giving more of herself to me, even if only for this moment.

Her moans are the sound of heaven, her eagerness to meet me halfway on each pump promising. She wants this as much as I do.

Our mouths meet as we fuck like two people who have two different missions. Hers, a release, and me, wanting to prove to her how right we feel together.

"You are so wet. It's because you want me. Want me to touch you, to fuck you, to give you something more." I slide in and out of her.

"Grayson, just shut up and give me this." She playfully and drowsily smiles at me.

I pull out of her and quickly turn her until she is facing the wall with her back to me. I guide her hands above her head and pull her hips back slightly. Re-entering her, I pull her close as we remain one. My fingers reach to stroke her, to drive every sensitive spot of hers crazy. I kiss the back of her neck and thrust harder.

Pressure builds below my torso, her yelps and breathing mixing as her hair falls over her face, and the realization that we are both going to get something out of this, even if only temporary relief, has me thrusting as deeply as I can. I need to feel as close to her as I can.

"Come with me. I'm almost there," I warn her.

"Mmm, me too, don't stop."

"Why the fuck would I do that? You're beautiful when you have that just-fucked look, and I tend to give that to you." I'm determined now to ensure she freefalls with me.

She leans back into me and turns her head, inviting me to kiss her. Our mouths fuse, and her wanting all I can give in this moment is sexy as hell. When her pussy pulses around my cock with our bodies completely connected, it's the final straw for me. I feel the jolt then unload inside of her.

The pressure eases, and my state of bliss is one that I've missed.

We're standing in her hallway next to the laundry room, two people completely sated from sex.

Our pulses are still beating quickly, I know because I feel hers as she stays in my arms. I kiss up her spine, her t-shirt be damned. Brushing her hair to one side, I kiss a line to her ear.

"Next time we do it in bed and I take my time with you," I whisper, satisfied, in a daze of pleasure before pulling out of her.

She turns around, and her face tells me she has other ideas.

…Ones that I may not like.

"So, this escalated too quickly," she tells me before leaning over and scooping up her jeans.

"I like a little escalation, but to be fair, I'm not sure he's that little." I grin.

She playfully slaps me. "Funny, funny. Be happy I ditched the idea for the swear jar, otherwise you would have just made my daughter rich with all your filthy words during sex."

It makes me chuckle under my breath.

"This can't happen again," she says.

"Hey, hey, hey," I try to calm her and cup her head with my hands. "We'll go slow."

She shakes her head in disagreement. "Grayson, what I said earlier is still all true. One orgasm doesn't change that. I can't let Rosie get attached for you, only for you to return to your life in two years. I can't do it again either."

I haven't thought about my life in the city once today, and I don't think I did yesterday either.

"I understand." I step away and grab my clothes to put on again, as it seems like round two is not on the agenda for today. "But I'm not going anywhere right now, and I can't stay away."

"Maybe you should try harder. *I* should try harder." She begins to walk away. "I need to clean up then go pick up Rosie. This was fun but... yeah, I've said my piece." Her tone is neutral.

As I watch her disappear into the bathroom to clean up the mark I left inside of her, I know this isn't the last of this conversation.

Because I will prove to her how wrong she is. We are exactly what each other needs.

9

GRAYSON

Helping Knox move a few crates of wine bottles and olive oil to the back of his truck from the barn, I'm grateful for the unexpected arm workout. It's a way to get out some frustration.

It's not that I'm frustrated with Brooke. It's more, it feels like she is waving a flag in front of a bull, which only hypes the animal up more. Not that I'm a bull, I consider myself a lean specimen, it's just… I'm hyped up, and I wouldn't put the urge to charge past me when a territorial feeling creeps up too.

It's only two days later, and I've lost sleep, burned my mouth with coffee, and my morning run was a bit more brutal than normal.

How am I supposed to stay away from her now that my tongue has swept across her lips, into her mouth, worked my way down her body then back up, and tasted her again?

I won't. Simple as that.

The sound of the bottles jostling in the box as I set it in the trunk reminds me to focus on the task, so I don't make Knox think I've lost my ability to do manual labor. I already get enough crap from him about not wearing my white button-down shirts anymore.

"You seem completely in your own world. Everything okay? Lucy driving you crazy?" Knox sets a crate down.

"She's fine. Well, I mean, she seemed a little distant after the party the other night but swears nothing happened." I shrug. I picked Lucy and Kendall up at 12:06—giving them six minutes past a generous curfew—and she seemed quieter than normal. Stormed off to her room when we got home. The next morning, she called me a martyr for not buying fresh lemon for hot tea so she could work on her skin complexion, so I thought we were back to business as usual.

"Hmm, I'll keep an eye on her when she comes to ride her horse later."

I lean over to pick up the last box. Knox will head to the Chicago suburbs to deliver the bottles to a few restaurants. We have a delivery company deliver to downtown Chicago, as it's easier.

After setting the last box in, Knox closes the door to the truck and leans against it, crossing his arms. I sense he's studying me.

"You know you can't hide it," he says as he kicks a pebble on the ground.

I prop myself against the truck and place a hand on my hip. "What would that be?" I play innocent.

"I don't believe for a second that a reunion drink at Rooster Sin led to nothing. Not with you and Brooke. Hell, people swear the ground there is magical or some shit like that—it affects people."

I grin at his opinion of the place. "Truthfully, nothing happened other than running into every citizen of Bluetop. Then with the storms coming through, we had the girls around."

Knox raises a brow at me and perks his head. "The girls? You make it sound like you've formed some kind of insta-family."

"It's not like that. We're just both tied down to people who depend on us."

He grumbles at me. "Oh boy, there's your problem. You see any human under the age of eighteen as anchors that tie you down. No wonder Brooke wants to keep the neighbors-only policy. Why invest time with someone who sees her kid as a burden?"

"Wait, that's not what I meant. I just meant that we had an audience then, so we weren't alone."

He steps away and shakes his head subtly in disapproval. "Then? You saw her again?"

I rub my neck and realize he sees through me. "I did."

"Really?" His voice raises slightly. "You went *there*? Already? I thought I had another week before I would need to remind you that sleeping with her is a horrible idea, considering we're all still wondering how committed you are to staying once Lucy is off to college. Not to mention, you hate cornfields and forests, and Bluetop is surrounded by Illinois's finest."

I laugh at his notion of me. "Right, Grayson the city boy, even though I grew up here and my share of Olive Owl is just as big as yours."

"You also left as soon as you got the chance. Even a beautiful and bright woman couldn't keep you here." He seems defensive and angry.

"What the hell is up with you? You act more like *her* brother."

"That's not it. I just think it's shitty the way you weren't there as a friend for Brooke when she probably needed that the most. She's done it all by herself with Rosie."

I adjust my posture and square off with him, as it feels like an argument where neither one of us will settle down until an external element forces us to.

"As my brother, I would hope you realize that it was fucking miserable learning that Brooke was pregnant and that the baby wasn't mine. What good would I have been to her being a jealous asshole who barely lived in his own condo because he was traveling all the time? Huh? Yeah, tell me what I could have offered as a mostly absent friend?" I shove him gently because this feels like another time in our lives when we were growing up rumbunctious and constantly challenging each other.

"Mostly absent is better than being completely absent. Yet, you stroll back into town and everyone welcomes you with open arms. Brooke may have forgiven you, but when this heads south, don't come to me." He pinches the bridge of his nose, his irritation in full swing.

We have always been this way with one another, coming down hard, and sometimes I thought it was jealousy bubbling under the surface. Of what? I'm not quite sure.

I step away to blow out a breath. "You know none of us can change the past, but here I am now, and I have no plans of hiding away in the house to stay out of everyone's path."

"Then step it up and think with your head and not your dick."

I throw my arms in the air, aggravated. "Maybe I am. Have you ever thought that maybe I know I'm going to have to grovel? And you know what? I fucking don't care, because she deserves someone who will crawl on their knees to prove they are worthy."

He scoffs a laugh. "And you're that guy? What the hell is with you two? You speak all of five minutes and suddenly you're on a mission? Is it because it's convenient?"

"It's not convenient, trust me, it's a confrontation. One that was always going to happen because she never left my head."

Knox looks at me with his eyes serious as I feel my nostrils flaring with my fists clenching at my sides.

"What the hell is going on out here, boys? I can hear you all the way upstairs with the vacuum cleaner on." Helen walks out of the bed-and-breakfast with a sweater that is far too seasonal for me.

Knox brings his hands up, indicating for her to calm down. "It's nothing. Just trying to knock sense into my older brother."

"I sure hope it's nothing. The last thing you need is guests showing up to find brothers, who are also the owners, arguing. I mean, there are worst things a young future bride could walk in on, if you know what I mean." She nudges my arm with her elbow and winks at me.

"Well, don't worry. Our conversation is done," Knox says. "Bennett is going to meet with the couple who are stopping by to plan for their wedding next month." He pulls his car key out of his pocket and heads to the driver's side. "See you round, Grays."

I roll my eyes at his sudden neutral tone that I would have appreciated to have the last five minutes.

Glancing to my side, I notice Helen batting her lashes at me as she waits for me to explain.

"Nice sweater, Helen, did the Hobby Lobby have a sale on sequins?" I ask, indicating to her purple flower.

She stretches out her sweater. "Really? You like it? Made it at Tuesday crafts with the ladies."

I can't even respond to that, as nothing about that sentence is interesting.

"I need to head out. Can you ensure there is lunch available tomorrow? I have a contractor coming out, and I want to discuss options for the extension of the barn," I mention as I swipe my phone to check for e-mails and the time.

"Sure. Must be nice being back and helping out here, no?" she asks as she follows me to my car not far away.

"Can't complain," I tell her, and it's the truth. I like making my own schedule, seeing firsthand what goes into running the winery and farm, and Christ, I haven't had this much fresh air on a daily basis in years.

All the more reason to explore what life here with Brooke would look like.

————

A FEW HOURS LATER, I have Lucy moping behind me as we walk out of the animal supplies store on Main Street. She is unusually quiet, and I'm beginning to wonder if something went down at the party over the weekend, or as much as I hate the thought crossing my mind, if it's her time of the month. Either way, when I asked if she wanted to head to this great burger place half an hour away, she said no, and that's a bad sign.

Her behavior is almost as puzzling as how I was volunteered to pick up a bag of feed for the chickens since the wholesaler delivered the wrong bag. But since my tense debate with Knox, I felt I needed to step up to the plate and show commitment to Olive Owl, even if it is a task that doesn't fall under my department.

"Ice cream?" I call back to Lucy.

"Do I look like I'm seven? I can't be bought with cookie dough ice cream and sprinkles." There's that moody tone that makes me smirk in amusement every time.

"Fine. Throw me a clue what her highness could possibly want to eat this evening?"

"Not really hungry," she replies, and I stop us in our tracks.

"You good?" I double-check as I glance over my shoulder to her and hope she'll throw me a bone. Talking to a wall with eyes gets kind of distorting after a while.

"Ugh, can we not do this here?" She's looking at her phone but glimpses up for a millisecond to take note of where we're standing.

Hell, I notice my error in that moment too. We are on the sidewalk near Kelsey's salon, and in the corner of my eye I see a familiar brunette whose watermelon smell is my downfall.

Brooke slowly approaches us along the sidewalk as she raises her sunglasses. Her eyes travel between me balancing a fifty-pound bag of bird food—literally—in my arms, and my sister who looks at her with admiration in her eyes.

"Hey, there," Brooke quickly greets us. Her eyes only briefly connect with my own before she turns her focus away from me. Avoidance is her tactic.

"Hey," I reply.

"Do you two need a minute?" Lucy asks. "This feels kind of weird, and I don't know if this is just adult communication or…"

"What?" Brooke quickly squeaks out. "Oh no, we are *totally* fine. What brings you guys to town?" She tries to smooth our conversation away from awkward, and for that I am thankful.

"Stuff for Olive Owl," I answer at the same time my sister says, "Dragged against my will."

I give everyone a closed-mouth smile at this situation. "Right, such a hard life when your brother offers you a road trip for a burger, ice cream, or anything you want for dinner."

"I said it already, I am *not* hungry." Whoa, the tone there is not appreciated.

Brooke angles her head to me so my sister can't see her facial expression. "Everything okay?" she mouths.

I shrug my shoulders as I re-balance the bag. We both glance back to my sister who has stepped away to take a selfie.

"I have no clue what's up with her. There are way too many options to choose from." I set the bag down, as I feel an opening to talk a little with Brooke.

"You?" I ask. "What brings you to town? Where's Rosie?" Because I'm kind of disappointed that the little preschooler isn't here to stare up at me, before pointing her little finger at something.

The corner of her mouth hitches up. "You always ask where she is when I'm alone. You know we aren't attached to the hip."

"Oh, I know." And what you get up to when you are alone is something I thoroughly enjoy.

"I have an hour between finishing work and needing to pick her up at preschool so thought I would cram in seeing Kelsey, since she had a leak in the roof from the storm the other day."

I scratch my cheek as I try to cover my grin forming. "A lot to talk about?"

I'm sure I am on the agenda.

Her eyes bulge out at me, as she knows me too well. "Don't even, Grays."

Ah, but her smile she is trying desperately not to let form tells me otherwise.

"Relax," I try to ease her. "I'm trying to be on good

behavior since I can't afford any setbacks today with that one." I indicate to my sister with my thumb hitching in her direction.

"She's sixteen, she goes through twenty moods in one day. I'm sure it's nothing."

"Hope so. She's been this way since the party."

Lucy rejoins us and slides her phone into her back pocket. "Can we go home? I have a lot of homework."

"Sure. I'm sure Brooke wants us out of her hair anyway." I lean over to pick up the bag of feed.

Brooke adjusts the purse strap on her shoulder. "It's fine. Just picking up nail polish for later with Rosie and Kelsey. Girls' night."

"That's cool," Lucy says softly.

Brooke looks at Lucy then puts a hand on her shoulder. "Join us."

"Really?" Lucy's mood suddenly begins to turn more positive.

"For sure," Brooke assures her before looking at me.

I mouth *thank you* and Brooke's mouth quirks out in that comforting subtle smile that represents the genuine caring person she is.

All the more reason that I am more than certain she deserves someone worthy of her.

And I am ready to get on my damn knees and crawl to her until she sees all our possibilities.

BROOKE

Putting the carton if ice cream back into the freezer, I smile to myself. Lucy just went home with fresh purple nails, plus a better mood after she confessed the guy she was interested in turned out to be more into the quarterback. Rosie is asleep in bed with a crown on her head, and Kelsey is pouring me a glass of white wine. But it's the pistachio-chocolate-chip ice cream that lights a little firefly inside me.

Grayson sent Lucy over with a carton of ice cream, and it just happened to be my favorite flavor. It's also only available at one of the two grocery stores in town, which means he made the effort to go the extra half mile.

Closing the freezer door, I'm greeted with Kelsey swirling the wine in her glass where she's sitting on top of the counter.

"Okay, Lucy is gone, so spill it. How deep are you in with Grayson Blisswood?"

I take my glass of wine and take a sip. "Let's just say, we-couldn't-even-make-it-to-my-bed deep."

Wine sprays out of her mouth before she sets her glass

down and drags her other hand across her chin. "Tell me not where I am sitting now?"

"No. Didn't even make to the kitchen either."

My facial expression goes in different angles as I wait for her to respond.

"So, you're back on?" Her tone is slightly confused yet very curious.

I stare blankly into my wine. "No. It's not a good idea."

"I'm not sure about that. If you are both so drawn together, then let fate lead the way. I mean, neighbors-only isn't a sustainable situation. You will literally cross paths with him on a daily basis, and don't tell me you would enjoy it if you push him away and have to see another woman leave his house."

My eyes dart up to look at my friend because that thought is not one I enjoy in the slightest. Already I feel my muscles coil from the mere idea of Grayson with someone else.

"I can't risk it with his fantasy of living a different life away from here. I have Rosie to think about. She can't get attached to the idea of me and him, only to be disappointed when he takes some job in New York or somewhere when Lucy is off to college."

Kelsey sighs as she plays with the cork of the bottle. "Isn't she going to get attached anyway since your lives interconnect already since, well, in case you missed it, he lives next door."

"Thanks for the reminder, but it's different when we're just friends. If he becomes more than that, to a three-year-old, she would associate him as her new father. Already at the grocery store she points out mommies and daddies who kiss."

"What about you? What do you want?"

I lean over the counter and prop myself up on my elbows. "There are a lot of things I want, but that doesn't mean it's good for me. Hell, I could swallow that whole tub of ice cream, doesn't mean I should."

"It's kind of cute that he remembers those little details about you. I mean, we all change since we were teenagers. *But* he got to know you as an adult too when you two couldn't keep your hands off one another a few years back. B, I think you really should give it a chance."

I purse my lips and let my jaw slide side to side. "I'm just going to take it one day at a time. I can't even process what I'm cooking for dinner tomorrow, let alone figure out my long-term strategy for dealing with Grayson Blisswood right now."

Kelsey smiles as she hops off the counter. "Keeping a Blisswood guy in line does take serious willpower." I feel like she is speaking from experience.

"How would you know?"

"Oh, uh, I don't. Just guessing." She grabs some of her hair to pull to the side as if she needs to occupy herself.

"Something you need to tell me?" Now my curiosity is sparked.

"Nope. Anyhow, I think you should just go with the flow. I'm away for a few days, so I'm sure Grayson can keep you occupied." She wiggles her brows at me.

"You have that conference, right?"

"Yeah, I'll be up in Detroit for a salon-and-spa expo. I'm kind of excited."

"You should be. I mean, your styling has landed in some awesome blogs lately." Kelsey often does the bridal hair and makeup for wedding parties at Olive Owl, and a few months back she did it for the bride of a big restaurant entrepreneur in Chicago, and since then she has been in high demand.

She grabs her purse to leave, and I follow her. "I hope you have a good time," I tell her.

Kelsey turns to me and smiles. "Thanks. But you have a good time too." She grabs my shoulders to pull me into a hug.

"Trust me, my life is a little chaotic with a toddler running around. Never a dull moment."

"All the more reason you should have fun too. Let him be your escape."

I laugh at her thought. "Sure, I will schedule in escape time with Grayson between folding laundry at nine and Rosie waking at three in the morning to crawl into bed."

Stepping back, we say our goodnights.

"Your escape, Brooke," she calls out when she's halfway to her car.

Waving her off, I debate if I should consider that there are other roads with Grayson that I should perhaps explore. Because he hasn't left my mind since the other day when his lips found mine then took me as if I'm the only one he will ever need.

———

LYING ON MY STOMACH, I open my drowsy eyes to glance at the time on my phone before the device plops to the ground. It's early afternoon, and I was sent home from work just before mid-morning break. The last few days my sinuses have been acting up, but now it feels like it may be a migraine.

There is no way I will be able to drive and pick up Rosie. Half of my head feels like it's going to explode.

Dragging myself up to sitting, I rub my head and begin to run through a list in my head of who can help me out. Normally, Kelsey is my savior, but she's out of town. Whoever helps me also needs a car seat in the back. I'm short on time because I overslept from my nap so I can't have Knox or Bennett swing by.

Normally in these situations one calls on their neighbor. Mine just happens to be Grayson.

I have no other option, and I know he's working from home, as I noticed his car parked out front earlier.

Letting out a calming exhale, I tap the call button on my phone. Every ring ups the ante, as I know inviting him to play hero is a mixed message for all of us.

"Hey." Grayson's tone is slightly surprised but equally concerned.

"Hey. Sorry to bother you, but I kind of need a favor and I'm out of options."

"Last resort. Now I feel *really* special."

I rub my head from how that must sound. "Not what I meant for it to sound like." Well, it is, but I'm trying to be polite.

"Are you okay?"

"Yeah… well… not really."

"Is it Rosie? Did something happen? What's wrong?" He sounds panicked, and it's kind of cute.

Ugh.

"No, uhm, she's fine. I'm at home actually and not feeling so great—"

"Do you need something?"

"Well, yeah, I really don't feel comfortable driving to pick Rosie up. Could you—"

"Help? Absolutely. I can go now." The eagerness in his tone is frustratingly sexy.

I stand and begin to pace around the living room. "Thanks. You'll need her car seat or to take my car. I'm sorry to disrupt your day."

"I'll come over now, and it's really not a problem."

"Okay."

It feels like my famous last words, but when I hang up the phone, my mission becomes finding something for my head before I send a message in the preschool app that Grayson has permission to take Rosie. It feels strange writing that, as if it's a glimpse of the life I always wanted with him.

The dream is where I bring him coffee while he draws designs at his desk. Dinners are filled with family time, and story time is a perfect ending to the day before we get our alone time together, where he would try and keep me quiet the only way I like.

My head moves slowly to the door to the garage where Grayson just let himself in.

He wiggles his key fob in the air, his jeans well filled out, his black t-shirt snug, and his eyes assessing me with worry. "Here I am."

"Thanks again."

He walks to me, and his hand instantly touches my arm. "What's wrong? Need me to get you something?"

"No, it's fine, just a headache. I'll take another quick power nap before Rosie gets home." I bite my lip, as I feel self-conscious in this vulnerable state, needing his help.

"Come on, B, want me to pick up some curly fries and a peanut butter shake on my way back?" He raises a brow and grins at me, knowing how much those are two of my favorites.

A smile forms. "Nah, it's okay. I'll figure out dinner and stuff later. I let the preschool know you can take Rosie and you aren't some crazy guy. I'm sure Rosie will be a little confused, but just give her Jelly and remind her you're taking her home. Oh, and don't let that lip-quiver thing fool you, it's her way of making it impossible to say no."

He rubs warmth into my arm. "Don't worry, I can remain

strong. How about you rest, and when we get back, I can take her to the playground or something. Lucy is at Olive Owl after school and Bennett will drop her off later."

"See? It's your free time, you don't need an energetic little princess ruining it."

His knuckle soothes my cheek with a few strokes before he steps back. "Not ruining it at all. So go sleep and I will text you when she's safe in the car, okay?"

The light of his eyes, almost bright, tells me that he truly means what he says. He isn't bothered at all by this inconvenience. Because it isn't an inconvenience at all to him.

He wants to help me.

Which weakens my resolve to the max.

11

GRAYSON

Staring into the rearview mirror, I see a set of big blue eyes staring at me in awe. I'm not sure Rosie has blinked much since I picked her up. At first, she was curious about me. She recognized me but wasn't quite sure what I was doing there. Then I leaned down and pulled Jelly out from behind my back and she stepped forward with ease.

Still, she isn't certain of what to make of this situation.

"You okay there, Rosie? We'll be home soon," I remind her as I drive my car. I put Brooke's extra car seat in the back of mine.

Rosie nods slowly and her little mouth closes when she swallows before her jaw drops low again. I can't get over her eyes that remind me of something I can't quite pinpoint. She is for sure Brooke's daughter, a spitting image. But Rosie's eyes, I don't know, they draw me in. It's familiar but so unique, nearly sparkly too. I guess that's possible when the whole world is a wonder.

"Hungry?" I ask to try and get more backseat participation in this conversation.

"Mommy always gives me a snack after school," she informs me.

"That makes sense, you must be starving from all that learning. Your mom needs a nap, so why don't you tell me what you normally have."

"Hmmm." She brings her pointer finger to her chin as if she is contemplating, and the kid looks like a future leader. "Apples and ice cream."

I grin to myself. "Ice cream? Really?" My skepticism is high.

"Uh-huh. Or nuggets."

I know this kid has me wrapped around her finger. It would be a crime to say no to that little face.

"How about we go for a snack and pick up something for your mom?"

"Milkshake?"

Wow, this kid is ballsy. "Maybe," I reply. In the mirror, I can see her disappointment by the fact that her lip curls and— oh fuck, is this the quiver thing that Brooke was talking about? I feel like I just made Rosie sad for life. "Fries." I'm literally negotiating with a three-year-old.

She nods with a smile, and I feel my own face stretch from a grin.

"Grays, you know Mommy a long time?"

"Yep. Since she was Lucy's age. We went to school together."

"Oh." She frowns, and it has me wondering why. "Aunt Kelsey says that you were Mommy's boyfriend, but my mommy doesn't have boyfriends."

I very much approve of that confirmation, but how do I get us out of this conversation?

"I… was your mommy's boyfriend."

"Aunt Kelsey says that Mommy is in trouble because of you. Why? What did Mommy do?"

I run my tongue inside my mouth from the direction of where this is going. "Was Aunt Kelsey smiling when she said that?"

"Yeah, and Mommy didn't seem scared."

This child may be my ticket to intel.

"I think you and I will become good friends, kiddo," I say as I look ahead to the upcoming traffic light.

———

Rosie runs ahead of me into the living room while I trail after her carrying the food and shakes.

"Mommy! We got the bestest surprise." She throws her arms out before jumping on the sofa where Brooke is lying with a blanket.

"Oh, yeah?" Brooke looks at her daughter before turning her attention to me and instantly noticing the food. "What's this?"

"She strong-armed me into a snack." I admit defeat as I set everything down.

Brooke laughs. "Uhm, that looks like a big snack."

"I know, but I thought you could use a good meal for some strength. Got your favorite." I hold up the shake.

"She gave you the almost-cry look, didn't she?"

"Yup. Fell for it hook, line, and sinker."

Brooke smiles to herself and gets up and walks to me before reaching out and taking the cup. I hold it a little extra longer to ensure our eyes meet and our fingers brush along each other, and her wry smile tells me she approves.

"I can't really say no to this. Thank you. I forgot to send you with some snack options for the car."

"Not a problem. Figured out how to win her over."

"Of course you did," she nearly mutters under her closed smile.

We get to work on laying the food out on the dining table and soon we have Rosie eating more ketchup than fries and stealing sips from our milkshakes.

"Grays said I can go to the playground. Can I?" Rosie asks with a mouthful of fries.

"Maybe tomorrow. I'm sure he's busy, and today we can watch a movie," Brooke suggests as she steals a fry.

"Come on, B, it's fine. Let me take her and you can rest. I can work on my pull-ups on the monkey bars. It'll be fun." I do my best to convince her with one of my coy grins. I really want to take Rosie, and I hate the idea of Brooke not getting more rest if that's what she needs.

Brooke scratches the back of her head. "I guess that's okay, if you insist."

"Least I can do for hyping your kid up on sugar. Help her burn it off." I lean back in my chair.

"Trust me, your daily workout doesn't hold a candle to what you are about to experience at the playground. She will wear you down beyond recognition." Her humorous look accompanies her warning.

"Really? This kid is like her mother; I think you also have that talent." I can't help but flirt the innuendo her way.

Brooke replies by giving me narrowed eyes. "Ha, ha." She turns her attention to Rosie. "Alright, finish your nuggets and then grab a sweater and you can show Grays your wildling ways."

A few minutes later, Rosie is in her room to grab a sweater, which gives Brooke and me an opportunity to be alone.

"Thanks again," Brooke says as she begins to clear the

table. "Go easy on the moms there. They aren't used to a Blisswood hanging around the playground, and I'm not sure their blood pressure is ready for it."

Smiling to myself as I lean back in the chair and cross my arms, I very much like the direction of where this conversation is going. "That's all favorable for me. So, tell me… do you and Kelsey always make a habit of talking about me or is it only when you can't get me out of your head? Or is it because you like trouble when I'm involved?"

Brooke freezes and her face turns a shade of red.

"Right, because you don't talk about me with your brothers?" She cocks a brow at me. "Neighbors, you and I are neighbors. No matter what our history is or if you play hero." It feels like she is talking more to herself than me.

"Relax, I'm just playing with you. And since I have been restricted to only doing so with words, then it's quite easy." I step toward her, causing her to move back. I've noticed my presence makes her extra, well, heightened in senses. My fingers reach out to brush a bit of her soft hair behind her ear. "Take it easy, have some time for yourself. I've got this," I softly remind her.

And just like that, her body melts. Her face presses into my hand and her lips brush against my palm. Maybe her body is acting out of habit from those years ago or I'm simply what she wants.

Before I have an opportunity to pull her against my chest to give her a comforting hug, Rosie comes running back into the room, causing us to quickly part.

"Mommy, Jelly is going to stay here. You need her." Rosie hands the stuffed animal over to Brooke who quickly kneels and hugs her daughter.

"Why thank you. I feel better already."

Rosie looks at me excitedly as she jumps in place. "Come on, Grays."

"Are we racing there, or do you want a piggyback ride?" I'm not sure why it all comes so naturally, the way to interact with her, but it does.

I've never thought about being a father except the three seconds four years ago in the pause of a sentence when Brooke told me she was pregnant. Those three seconds flashed before me, and all thoughts were surprisingly positive.

"Uh-oh, your back is going to regret that offer." Brooke grins, and we both look at one another in agreement that I'm about to be worn out.

———

AND AN HOUR AND A HALF LATER, I return with a child who has schooled me on the slide and insisted my pushing skills on the swing were too slow, but I was afraid I would push too high. Rosie's energy level makes taming a teenager feel like a walk in the park.

Carrying Rosie on my shoulders, we walk up the driveway to where Brooke is sitting on the bench swing on her porch, wearing an oversized sweater. She has been watching us since her head perked up as soon as we were in her sight.

I can't help but notice that Brooke is observing the scene, and she's lost in thought. The corner of her mouth twitches as if it wants to smile but something is holding her back. She plays with the charm on her necklace, the way she used to do when she was nervous.

But her smile spreads as soon as we're within speaking distance.

"Where should I deposit this one?" I nod my head up to the child on me.

"I guess she'll need a bath. How about you set her down and she can watch the tablet for a little while," Brooke says as she helps Rosie off my shoulders.

"Yeah," Rosie answers simply before heading inside, and something tells me she knows where to find the device.

Brooke tucks her hands into the back of her jeans, and we look at one another. She seems stuck on words, and I wait patiently to see what she says.

She tilts her head to the swing, and I take that as my indication to follow her. We both settle onto the bench swing without words, and she angles her body in my direction by propping her elbow against the back.

"Thank you, really. It looks like she had a good time." She glances through the window to check that Rosie has grabbed the tablet and is sitting on the sofa.

"And you look like you may be disappointed in that fact," I tell her.

She laughs softly. "It doesn't make it any easier. You've gained a new fan."

There's a pause in our conversation as we both get lost in each other's eyes, the moment, hell, the feeling that this seems easy and a step toward something right.

"I don't know how to do this. I remember you as my first everything, including my first broken heart, but even worse, I remember you as the guy who grew into a man who mastered a few skills and is so damn determined. But the problem is that he doesn't know what he is determined for."

My head retreats back slightly as I take in her words, her fears. "I think you should give me a chance to prove you wrong."

Her lips quirk out before she drops her head into her hand. "Grays, I can't think right now."

Touching her hand, I interlace our fingers, and she doesn't pull away. She has surrendered to me in a way. "Then don't think."

"Oh, man, I shouldn't have gotten you involved today. I've just complicated things." She glances up to the sky then back to me.

"I'm happy you called. Are you feeling all good now?"

A coy smile forms on her lips. "I am, or at least I was until I saw you carrying my daughter on your back, because that isn't great for my keep-Grayson-Blisswood-in-my-neighbors-only plan."

"You know you don't have a chance at keeping me in that category."

"Maybe."

"She's a good kid, Brooke. You've done really well, just like I knew you would."

The corner of her mouth curves up from appreciation. "I try. I got lucky on the daughter front so it's easy most of the time." She tilts her head in a humorous manner. "Well, until she demands cookies and a playhouse."

I laugh at her reference. "She may have mentioned the need for a playhouse a few times this afternoon."

"Yeah, I'm actually going to get her one. I was looking online, you know those plastic log cabins that you puzzle-piece together—"

I interrupt in a heartbeat. "No way. Let me make one for her."

"What?" Her voice screeches slightly.

"Designing buildings is my thing, I'm sure I can master a playhouse. Come on, are you really going to say no to this? It means you don't have to build it yourself."

She yanks her hand away from me and playfully puts on a surprised face. "I'm sure I can build a playhouse." She doesn't sound believable.

I'm kind of excited by this. I can already imagine where to put the door and windows, I guess we need to paint it too.

"I mean, nothing crazy. My parents may sell this place at some point, which means I'll have to move out. So don't go overboard."

"Then it's settled. Now, I should head out, Lucy's home soon. Any gossip you can share on that front?"

"Not a chance... Grayson, I don't know what to say except thank you."

We both stand and I touch her shoulders so she can't escape my gaze. "You don't need to say anything. I'm here for you, whatever you need, *anything* you need."

Yeah, offering to be her fuck-buddy is not my ideal win, but it's an in to persuade her that we can be more.

"Anything, huh?" She licks her lips as she tries to hide her entertainment with me. "Listen, can we just try and do the friends thing?"

I blow out a deflating breath and my eyes narrow in to study her. "If you change your mind, you'll let me know?"

"I assume you would need to know to be part of the equation," she teases me with a little smirk.

I roll my eyes at her humor. "Well... say goodbye to Rosie for me. Just call if something comes up. I'm here, and I'm not going anywhere."

And I know that last word is what has her mind twisting into a million thoughts.

Turning to walk away, I hesitate to move farther. Glancing over my shoulder, I see she hasn't moved. "You know, I don't really know how to stay away from you."

"You did it for twelve years," she deadpans a truth that I

know hurts for her, and it does for me too, even if it's my own doing.

"…And I would spend another twelve years to make up for it."

Her mouth parts open but no words come out. We have nothing left to say in this moment because we both have a lot to think about.

She will toss and turn all night with thoughts of me, and I'll be busy designing the best damn playhouse this state has ever seen, because I want to prove to Brooke that she has me.

12

BROOKE

L ooking out my kitchen window, I realize I've been rinsing the lettuce for what seems like minutes, as I am lost in a daze in the scene in front of me. Grayson and Bennett are busy hammering away at a house fit for a princess. The whole week, Grayson sent me blueprints of his ideas which were all beyond over the top, and this morning he went to pick up supplies.

Kelsey took Rosie and Lucy to the grocery store since we're trying to keep Rosie out of the way, and I forgot the avocados for the salad. I figured offering dinner is the least I could do, since they're making a mansion, not a house.

Finally, I turn the faucet off and try to gather some composure, as I am confident that I may start drooling soon. My predicament is made worse when Grayson glances up from drawing on the wood with a pencil and winks at me.

Since he helped me out with Rosie the other day, I've been distracted. Seeing him with Rosie melted my heart into a puddle and then was glued back together by his mere presence. He's good with her, and the way he made me feel like I wasn't an inconvenience to him was surprising.

He has made his intentions clear, and the ball is in my court.

Glancing up at the sound of the garage door opening, I see the girls come in with a few bags.

"We're back. Got a little more than avocados. I thought we could get some daiquiris on the go," Kelsey announces proudly.

"You brought my three-year-old and sixteen-year-old neighbor liquor shopping?" I feign concern.

"Relax, Lucy seemed to know the aisle better than me," Kelsey informs me, and we both shoot our gaze at Lucy, who gives us a shrug.

"Don't be like that. I'll be back, need to charge my phone," Lucy says before departing.

Rosie quickly runs to the sliding doors and looks out into the backyard; she tries to open the door but has no luck, as I locked it. Walking to her, I jiggle the lock and warn her, "Don't get in the way. You can watch or play with something else, okay?"

Returning to the middle of the kitchen, Kelsey is busy setting up the Bluetooth and throwing on some tunes. I get to work on unpacking the bags, and we both gravitate our eyes in the direction of outside.

She snorts a laugh. "I think having two Blisswood guys building here just increased your property value. Notice the old lady peering over the fence?"

"This isn't good. Really not good." I can't help grinning.

"Not bad either. I mean, this is quite the view."

I glance to the side and see that she is eyeing the scene with a little extra attention.

"You okay? You seem… invested."

Quickly she straightens her posture and returns her gaze

to me. "Nope. Not. So, shall we do strawberry or lime drinks?"

Huh, something is going on there for sure.

"I'll take the guys beers," I suggest and grab a couple from the fridge.

When I make it outside, I see that Rosie is sitting next to the design of her playhouse.

"Mommy, Grayson said I can sup-supr—"

"Supervise. She's supervising," Grayson explains as he points for Bennett where to drill in a screw at a corner.

"Well, if the boss lets you," I tell him, "I have some beers, and Kelsey seems to be on a mission to make something stronger. Your sister will be back, she had a phone crisis." I hold up the bottles.

Both brothers pause in their work and give me that charming smile that is basically heaven and hell merged into one.

"Shi...ucks," Bennett begins but then notices my daughter so changes his word. "If Kelsey is on drink duty, then this could get messy."

I hand them their beers, and again I wonder what the hell is going on. Since when does Bennett know about Kelsey's escapades?

"Thanks," Grayson says. "We should be done today and can paint another day. I can take Rosie with me to pick out the colors," he suggests before taking a long sip.

"Purple," Rosie pipes up.

"Surprising," I state then return my focus to Grayson. "Uhm, this special pasta I make is okay?"

"Absolutely. Lucy has been going on about it for weeks."

"I know, it's basically my version of Hamburger Helper, so I'll teach her. A trade-off, right?"

"As long as it keeps Lucy under our noses, you can teach

her knitting, for all I care," Bennett mentions and focuses his eyes on the kitchen window. "I'll go wrangle her in... Lucy, I mean."

I watch him walk off and then look at Grayson, confused, and raise my finger in the direction of the kitchen. "Is he also acting weird or is it my imagination?"

"Also? Ah, maybe he and Kelsey are..." His face forms a funny expression.

"Huh. Anyhow, thanks for doing this. This is just beyond what I imagined, and Rosie is excited. You really made a super fan."

"Just her?" He gives me a cocked brow and that slow grin spreads like wildfire to all parts of my body.

Clearing my throat, I ignore his attempt to flirt. "So, uhm, salad. Right, dressing on the side? Yeah, I should do that, so everyone can pick what they want," I ramble, which only makes him more entertained.

"I like when you're at a loss for words around me. Shows me that you're debating what to do with me." He crosses his arms and flashes a quick smile to Rosie who peers up at him from where she's sitting on the ground.

Now I just turn my head as my eyes roll ruefully. I am slightly aggravated, in a spirited way, with his persistence. "There are many options, and trust me, not always in your favor."

His jaw flexes, but he's still enjoying my words because he doesn't mind a challenge.

"Come on, Rosie, want to help me make dinner?" I offer my hand to my daughter.

"Grays is staying for dinner?" Her voice is full of hope.

"Yeah, kiddo, just like I told you. Everyone is staying, they're working up an appetite."

As we begin to walk away, I hear Grays mutter something

to me as he touches my arm gently. "Trust me, dinner isn't going to satisfy the appetite I've worked up."

Now I can't help but smile as I playfully push him. "This feels like we're seventeen again."

"Mommy, you shouldn't push Grays."

"I was playing," I answer her.

"But I have to go in time-out when I push."

Grays rumbles a chuckle under his breath. "Don't worry, Rosie, I'll make sure your mommy has a time-out under my watch."

I can only shake my head as Rosie and I work our way back inside.

———

THE SQUEAL OF a teenager nearly pierces my eardrums. "Really? I can take my driving test soon?" Lucy excitedly bounces in her seat upon hearing the news that Bennett broke to her and shocked us all, including himself, where we're sitting at the dining table.

"Heaven help us," Grayson states.

Kelsey and I can only smile at the scene in front of us.

"I'm going to have to start looking into outfit options for my license photo," Lucy declares.

"We've got you," Kelsey confirms, and I nod.

"Well, your outfit isn't a priority. Let's maybe try parallel parking a few more times, your instructor says you need to work a little more on that." Bennett leans over to grab the bowl of bread.

"I can do that. Maybe Tuesday when I'm at Olive Owl?" Lucy asks, and Bennett nods in agreement. "Cool. Can I be excused? I have a live to do in twenty minutes."

All the adults look at one another, confused.

"Social media," she clues us all in.

"Sure. Just keep your t-shirt choice respectable, and remember, what goes online is in the universe forever," Grayson reminds her.

Lucy's head moves in a way that tells me attitude is about to be paired with her words. "Oh, you mean like photos on high school walls of couples who win crowns."

Bennett and Kelsey immediately look at one another, trying to contain their laugh.

"Yikes, she just schooled you," Bennett grins.

"Wow, dragging me into this. Fun." I flex my jaw from the discomfort of it.

"Just stating a fact." Lucy stands and pivots then stalls. "Grays, can you bring me home some brownies later?"

"Yes, your highness," he answers with a little salute.

While Lucy leaves, I help Rosie off her seat and tell her that she can go sit and watch TV quietly.

The adults all resettle at the table and eye one another.

"So, Grayson," Kelsey begins as she holds her drink firmly in her hands. "How does it feel to be back? Itching to return to the city?"

"It feels slightly like a time warp but also different this time around." He quickly glances my way.

"It's good to have you back." Bennett affectionately slaps his brother's back.

"At least one of my sibling's feels that way," Grayson replies in good humor.

"Kind of funny being all in the same room again. Last time was, what, when you came back to visit your freshman year of college?" Kelsey tries to calculate a timeline in her head. "I missed the whole reunion four years ago."

I choke on my drink and slowly draw my eyes up to study everyone looking at me.

"Don't think that was a planned reunion." Bennett smirks to himself.

"Thanks, Kelsey, for that," I mutter. "Anyway, how is the wine-tasting event next weekend coming along?" I change the topic to save us all.

"Sold out," Bennet says, "and we're going to add another to the calendar. Soon, we'll need to expand the main house for more rooms for the bed-and-breakfast."

"I guess you know someone who could help design that," I say and glimpse at Grayson.

"I don't know. Playhouses may be my new calling. Tree-houses are next." Grayson leans back in the chair.

A silence takes over the table.

"Thanks again for doing the playhouse," I tell the brothers. "And thanks, Kelsey, for keeping Rosie occupied."

"Any time. I would love to stay, but I have an early morning tomorrow with the insurance guy coming to assess the leak. Hopefully tornado season isn't so bad this year," Kelsey explains, and I feel like this is her tactic to get Grayson and me alone.

Bennet stands. "I should head out too, have to respond to some bookings for a wedding in a few months at Olive Owl."

Grayson moves his plate to the side. "You don't need to resort to trapping us alone. We're past that. But I will help Brooke clean everything up."

"Sure, if that's what you want us to believe. I mean, you've both kind of been eyeing one another the whole dinner, even the sixteen-year-old picked it up," Kelsey informs us matter-of-factly.

I feel my face burning.

"Ah, how I haven't missed your boldness, Kelsey." Grayson also stands and gathers a few plates.

After everyone bidding one another goodbye, I get to work in the kitchen while Grayson clears the table. For the most part, we're too busy actually cleaning to head into deep conversation. But when he hands me the last plate for the dishwasher, I know our night is going to turn.

"Here you go."

"Thanks. Do you want me to put leftovers in a container so you and Lucy have something for tomorrow?"

His hand finds his heart. "Can't say no to that."

Taking in the moment, I enjoy having him here. It gets lonely doing housework by yourself. Having him around, although distracting, is a good feeling. But that's Grayson— he's like honey that runs down into corners you didn't know you have and absolutely gets sticky and stuck.

Turning so my back is leaning against the counter next to him, we stand side by side.

"So, beyond building infrastructure for toddlers, the past few years, did you get to do all the projects you wanted?" I'm curious, or maybe I just want confirmation that we both went down our correct paths in life.

"Sure. Had a project out in Seattle, helped design a hotel down in Miami, a new bank in Denver. They kept me busy." There is pride in his voice, but it's laced with an undertone that I can't quite figure out.

"But?"

He side-eyes me, with his tongue running along his inner cheek. "I forgot you know me too well."

I nudge his arm with my shoulder, encouraging him to continue.

"I think… I think I was always missing something."

His eyes connecting with my own makes my stomach spiral with hope. I open my mouth, but no words come out.

"What I said the other week…" he begins.

"You mean offering me *anything*." I flash my eyes to him.

A wry smile forms on his mouth. "Yeah, that. But I just want to make it clear that going slow is an option too. Despite a three-year-old bossing me around that her playhouse should have double doors, I'm not scared." He looks over to Rosie who is about to pass out on the sofa with cartoons on the screen. "I get it. I do. She's your number-one."

"I'm hers too."

"As you should be. But I am hoping that you both let me in."

His words are everything I want to hear; it's reassuring and a promise. Grayson Blisswood is a man of his word, even if you don't want to hear it. He never promised me a future at eighteen, so if he says he wants to try, then you better believe he will try. He doesn't bullshit.

Holding my finger up to stop him, I swallow. "Do you think you can stay for a little? I mean, can you wait until I get Rosie to bed?"

"Yeah, want me to help with something?"

"No, she is literally almost asleep. Just make a coffee or something. I'll try and be quick."

He nods gently, and I feel a current of nerves shoot through me. Because I'm beginning to think that I should take him up on his offer. Something is better than nothing, and right now, the air between us is too thick with want for us to be able to breathe normally.

For the next five minutes of soothing my daughter to sleep, I admire her little fingers. She was so tired from the excitement that we skipped brushing teeth and putting on pajamas, and instead I only took her sweater off.

Taking these moments, I think of all the possibilities and acknowledge that I never thought that letting Grayson back into my life would be the exact thing we need. It's a complete leap of faith, a gamble. But even gamblers sometimes win.

By the time, I return to the kitchen, my mind is set on a plan. One that makes sense to me, because wondering what could go wrong is just as painful as having nothing at all.

His eyes flick up to me, as he was staring at the floor with ankles and arms crossed. I bet he could drill a hole in the floor with his intense look. I'm sure he was wondering why I asked him to wait.

But making him wait, making me wait, that's just us.

Stepping into his space, I reach out to allow my fingers to crawl up his shirt-covered chest. I feel the thrum of his heart under my fingertips, my breath rapidly charging up because I know how he will answer me.

"The anything you mentioned." I mischievously give him a look before focusing on my fingers walking up to his shoulder. "Slow. We keep it between us for now." Before I can continue, his arms wrap around me and his mouth slams onto mine.

His hands quickly roam up my body until he is cupping my face. "Whatever speed you want. You set the rules. Well, outside of the bedroom." He's already nipping the corner of my mouth before he dives in to capture my lips again.

And as much as I hate to push him back, my mouth struggles to part, but I need to clarify. "What if slow is not going past first base for a *long* time." My arm hooks around his shoulders as I watch his face freeze slightly to study if I'm serious or not.

He lifts me up in a swift move and plants me on the kitchen counter. A sound escapes the back of his throat. "Then… I'll wait." Yikes, I hear the struggle in his voice.

I can't help but giggle softly. "Good thing I was testing you, because your face right now."

He groans playfully as he cradles and tips back my head in his hands. He moves slowly in to meld his mouth with my own.

A slow kiss that is agony for the desire between my legs. His tongue reminds me that he remembers my every inch.

And when he begins to kiss a line down my neck, and I get a glimpse of the juice box on the opposite counter, I'm reminded that we need a plan of action.

"Grays," I attempt to bring his attention back to eye level, and when I finally succeed, I see the desire in his eyes. It's a flame that may burn down the goddamn house.

"Rosie is here."

"And? She's sleeping." He moves in to tease that delicate patch just below my ear.

My hands intervene now to create some space. "We... well... I've never... not when she's home."

That grabs his attention in full force, and he plants a hand on the counter on each side of my body. "Wait, are you telling me that no other guy has been here since Rosie?"

I look away to avoid his gaze, as I suddenly feel shy. "Not since the other week when some guy took me against the hallway wall. Now don't get cocky."

A smirk spreads on his face that feels like he owns me, and I'm not complaining the slightest. "That fact you just dropped is making me feel quite territorial right now. You're mine, and it's hot. Let's go to your room."

I have to smile at his one-track mind. "What if she wakes or walks in on us? It will confuse the hell out of her."

His eyes go wide. "B, don't you remember the days when I would sneak into this very house? I doubt I've lost my skill to keep you quiet too." Before I can even answer, he hoists me over his shoulder and shushes me as I squeal.

It doesn't take long for me to know that he is taking us straight to the direction of my room.

He has a point to prove.

13

BROOKE

When he sets me on the bed, he quickly moves to close my door gently. I perch on the edge of the mattress and watch as he approaches me with hungry eyes, and instantly he is next to me on the bed, pulling us to lie down.

On our sides, we entangle with my leg propping over his and his hand resting on my hip. His throbbing dick presses against my middle as our mouths seal together.

We moan as our breathing grows ragged. His scent of wood, I know, will stay on my sheets.

Tugging on his shirt, I make my intentions clear what direction this night is going. For a second, we part so he can whip his shirt off.

"Mmm, more." I grip his belt, and I hear a low rumbled chuckle.

"That's my line," he answers, with his hands running up my shirt until he cups my bra. "Off, all of it."

Sitting up, he helps peel my clothing off until I'm down to my panties. We both stare at one another with a smirk of anticipation.

"Beautiful," he remarks, and his temporary praise quickly turns to demand. "Now lie down," he commands, and at the same time, he helps me by swiftly landing his lips on mine and keeping me occupied as he leads me back until my head is on the pillow.

Grays, as my first love, was patient, albeit always encouraging us to try new things, but sweet.

Grays as the guy I hooked up with four years ago was a man with a craving, a set plan of what he wanted to do with me, fun with someone familiar.

Grays now is all those things rolled into one, and this time there is a sentimental undertone with every touch, every glance, every kiss.

This is different.

It causes me to gasp extra hard when the feeling of his fingers grazing along my damp panties brings me into this moment.

His lips brush along my cheek. "Speak to me, B," he whispers tentatively.

"It's nothing. Just kind of can't believe we're here again," I softly reply, with my fingers entangling into his hair that is equal parts soft and perhaps rough from the sawdust.

The corner of his mouth tugs up from my words before he slowly kisses a trail down from my chin to my stomach, where his eyes peer up at me with a warning.

"It's the only way it was going to go, sweetheart."

I can't help but let a laugh escape. It's such a feel-good, shake-you-to-the-core kind of laugh. My body arches up underneath him from the enjoyment. Because Grayson Blisswood saying sweetheart is the most utterly ridiculous yet overly swoony thing he could do. It's almost like a Southern drawl graces his tone, and that's the funny part—we're in northern Illinois. Southern charm doesn't exist here.

"Ah, that still gets to you." He begins to tickle my belly with his stubbled chin and tip of his nose,

"Maybe," I play coy, but I'm almost hysterical.

He quickly slithers up my body to slam his mouth over mine to shut me up, before he murmurs against my lips. "Shh, we have to be quiet, remember?"

Our eyes connect, and as much as he is teasing me, there is sincerity in his sentiments. He knows it's important to me that we don't do anything to upset Rosie.

Softly, I nod.

"Good. Now keep your hands by your head, as you'll need the pillow." He returns to the destination he wanted before my laughter.

"Why?"

"Because you need to be able to muffle your mouth when I make you come with my tongue."

And before I can retort, he's peeling off my panties, and his mouth is placing butterfly kisses on my inner thighs as his hands hold my hips down and he lies on his stomach.

The cold air hitting my clit as he opens my folds makes me extra sensitive, as I am already revved up with need for him. His warm tongue licking up my slit makes me feel like I am flooding from want.

Oh. My. Fuck.

I forgot how he has this little trick where his teeth and tip of his tongue nip at my bundle of nerves. My entire body feels like fire, and I curve up into his mouth which only causes him to grunt in pleasure.

Yep. Need the pillow to block my overpowering moan from escaping my mouth.

He strokes me and then slides his tongue inside of me. He feels relentless, as if he is worshipping my pussy, and it makes me dizzy.

I'm convulsing and shaking under him in no time, and he rests his tongue on my clit for slow circles until I come down.

Grayson doesn't give me much time to regather my thoughts before his mouth, covered in my arousal, molds over my nipple and his hand kneads my breasts.

In a haze, I feel as if I'm floating. "So good," I murmur.

He answers me in moans, as if feasting on me is the ultimate pleasure in his life.

I touch his shoulders and hook my fingers under his chin to guide his gaze up to mine, to center us. This all feels one-sided—no complaints—but we are going into this as two.

"Lie on your back," I rasp and bite my bottom lip in anticipation.

His eyes light up with approval, and he obliges, with his eyes never leaving me.

Scooting onto my knees, I position myself next to his middle, and my hands slide his boxer briefs down. His hard, smooth cock stands at full attention, and just the sight causes a wave a desire in me to grow.

My hand grips his length as I work in smooth strides up and down, watching his eyes hood closed, his sounds stuck in his throat.

"Get on me," he requests.

"Nuh-uh, Mr. Blisswood, I have other ideas," I taunt him.

The grin gracing his mouth is purely sinful as his hand grips the hair on the back of my head.

"B, I'm nearly done for already if you keep this up, and I don't want to relive when I was a teenager right now."

Raising a brow to him, I dare him. "I think I'll keep it up."

He ruefully shakes his head at me as my mouth encloses around his cock. The taste of pre-cum settles on my tongue, and I take more of him. It's been a *long* time since I have done anything like this, and Grayson is well-endowed. It doesn't take long for my gag reflex to hit, and I retreat back slightly.

I glide my tongue around and up, finding a rhythm, humming my enjoyment.

"As much as I want to come inside your mouth, I need you on top of me." His low gravelly tone seethes with heat and lust.

Popping my mouth off him, I swing a leg over him to align myself on top of him. I'm dripping wet so he will slide right in.

Again, we pause, and our eyes catch for their own private conversation—it's acknowledgment.

He gently raises himself until he props himself on his forearms, facing me.

"Quiet. We'll stay quiet," he promises.

With that, I slide down and he presses up and instantly we are lost in one another.

I lean my mouth down and his tips up so we can connect through a kiss as he moves inside of me. Our arms wrap around one another.

My sensitivity heightens as every pump presses the right button inside of me.

We move in sync, everything entwined.

Until he flips us, so I'm on my back and he's above me, still inside of me.

"I've got you," he reminds me as my toes dig into his ass and my knees fall out, widening our angle.

His one hand encircles my wrist to pin down to the mattress and his other arm holds his body weight.

Ruffled sounds escape me on every grind.

"Shh," he playfully whispers. "Either keep your mouth on mine or bite into my shoulder."

My eyes widen, and then I realize he is dead serious.

"I'm already there," I begin but land my teeth on his shoulder to cover the roaring moan needing to escape from me as I pulse around his cock.

Pulling back, I look at him, slightly shocked, and he just gives me a reassuring grin before chasing his own release as he nuzzles his head into my neck.

Then we lie there.

Him and me.

Slightly sweaty, completely satisfied, a mess of two people who always find a way to reconnect.

It takes a minute or two before he pulls out of me, and he lies on his back, inviting me to crawl into his arms as he stares at the ceiling.

Adjusting my body, I place a gentle kiss on his pecs before my fingers begin to draw patterns on his skin.

"I hope I didn't leave a mark on your shoulder." I look up to him with my cheek pressed against him.

"I hope you did." His lips quirk out, and his hand begins to stroke my hair.

"Slow, right?" I double-check.

"What does that entail exactly?"

"Uhm, no sleepovers, since Rosie does still wake in the middle of the night sometimes. Not until we get to that stage."

He jostles and moves to his side so he can hover his gaze over me. "Like, secret dating?"

"Kind of." I doubt my answer.

"What about a date this week?"

"I need to get a sitter."

"I have a teenager back at the house that I can ground, we're good to go."

I swat him with my hand. "Don't do that. Lucy will resent us."

"You're right. But I think she's too smart for us. So really, we're keeping it all a secret from Rosie."

"*And* the town. Last thing I need is everyone watching my every move. The other week at Rooster Sin already caused enough of a stir. I couldn't pick up bagels from the bakery without ten questions from Sally-Anne," I acknowledge with a blown-out breath.

"Ah, but keep them guessing, it's fun. Okay, and what else?" He lets the back of his finger glide along my skin between the valley of my breast down to my belly button.

I pause and think about what I should be clear on.

"Can we just see where this goes? We kind of have lost time to catch up on, and we have to be super certain before... For now, you are our neighbor Grayson to Rosie, okay?"

He tucks a strand of hair behind my ear. "Okay."

"Thank you."

"Don't thank me yet. I don't plan to be a gentleman in waiting for that date. I will be relentless as hell. So let me arrange something."

I can't help but beam a smile. "Okay."

"We need to stop saying okay. We're more than that." He moves to sitting and scans for clothing.

Following suit, I sit up and grab my shirt. I would much rather lie around in his, but sleepovers are not in the equation right now.

Watching a man re-dress after sex only refuels my pent-up energy. It's a confirmation of what we just did, the image of a man satisfied.

He leans down to kiss me softly on the lips.

"Here we go, Brooke, you and me, another round, and this time we'll get it right."

My heart swells at his words. "Hopefully."

One quick peck more and he is heading to my bedroom

door. "Don't worry, I remember how to escape without notice. Sweet dreams."

And just like that, I let Grayson back into my life.

We have some navigation ahead of us, which causes me to huff a breath as I fall back onto the bed, the smell of sawdust and sex invading my senses.

A little twinge inside my soul reminds me that if we have any chance at all that I need to tell him my deepest secret I have never let escape my mouth. The doubt that haunts me as much as it's a hope.

14

GRAYSON

K nox looks up from his BLT sandwich in front of him. We're in the dining room at Olive Owl. His brow is arched, and his look is curious. "You're whistling like a fool."

"Is that a problem?" I say as I grab my iced tea.

"It's a sign that I should be worried." He continues with his skepticism as his eyes draw a line up and down my body, as if he's studying me for a clue.

But any person with a brain could figure out by looking at me that I'm in a fantastic mood. The moment Brooke asked me to wait in the kitchen, I knew she wanted to talk about us. And by the time she mentioned the words *try* and *slow*, my entire body was on fire with a need to show her how I very much approve of her changing her policy.

I throw a potato chip at him. "We're not all grumpy like you."

He freezes, flexes his jaw, then laughs humorously to himself. "Don't give me the bullshit that I'm a moody asshole. I just recognize when my brothers are under the influence of a female."

"Can't complain."

The sound of Helen walking to our table draws our attention and two plates filled with lemon bars lands in front of us. "Thought I would bring my extra batch to you boys. Need anything? Otherwise, I'll head out soon."

I offer her a smile. "Thanks, and these look good. Still using lemons from your tree?"

She seems nearly giddy that I remembered. "Yes, we planted a new tree last year too." She touches my shoulder and lowers her voice. "Don't tell Sally-Anne but I'm thinking of entering my pie in the competition at the fair."

"Oh, Helen, you devil. Sally-Anne better watch out then." I throw in the charming tone.

Knox just rolls his eyes. "You two are peas in a pod today."

"It's good to see Grayson a little chipper. May do you some good too," Helen nearly scolds him.

"Ignore him. Thanks for the lemon bars," I tell her.

"No problem. Oh, I see Coach Dingle." She waves at the man through the window. "He's picking up an order of wine and jams."

"I'll get it," Knox mentions before disappearing from his seat.

"You know the coach really is a saint in this town. Giving all those boys direction and putting our town on the map for sports. Your father donated to the team, always helped Dingle with team BBQs too," Helen points out before turning her head as Coach arrives at the dining area.

"Grays, good to see you again. Had a chance to think about my offer?" He grins hopefully.

I stand to shake his hand before I awkwardly scratch the back of my neck.

"I've been a little busy and occupied." Understatement of the century.

"I'm having a team dinner at my place next week. Come over, even if it's just for free burgers." He knocks my arm with his shoulder to encourage me.

"I guess it's hard to say no to free burgers."

In the corner of my eye, I see Knox return with a crate full of goods in his arms.

"Perfect. Just what I came for. You boys planting pumpkins this year for the fall?" Coach Dingle claps his hands together.

"Absolutely, it's becoming one of our main products since Midwest wine can only get so far with our winters," Knox informs him as he sets the box down on the ground.

"Look forward to it. Now, this is a quick pick-up, Rosemary will kill me if I don't mow the grass today. We'll see you next week, Grays, five pm sharp, and feel free to bring a plus-one." Coach winks at me before bending down to collect the box.

"I'll see you out," Helen offers.

"Thanks for the order," Knox says simply.

With Coach and Helen out the door, I'm faced with my brother, his arms crossed.

"Is there a plus-one?"

"In a way, yes, not exactly public," I admit as Knox and I sit down again at the table.

"Wow, you build a playhouse and she lets you back in."

I scoff a sound and wonder why he's giving me a hard time. "Think what you want, I'm allowed to have a life."

"Oh, that we know. You've been doing it for twelve years. And for the record, if you two live happily ever after then great, because who doesn't love a reunion."

The way he says that, I feel like there may be something

inside him that he pines for, but I've never been able to figure out what.

"It's time. The universe has given me every sign that this is our chance. I want to give Brooke and me another try, but there isn't much to try because it feels like we can pick up exactly where we left off, that's just us."

"*Except* there is also Rosie and Lucy," Knox corrects me.

Leaning back in my chair, I don't sigh or have an internal conflict or worry. Instead, I calmly smile and answer with the damn truth. "I know, and I'm not complaining. In fact, maybe it makes it all better. Rosie and Lucy give us the brakes when needed so we don't go too fast, and even though I could go pedal to the metal on this, I know it's better slow. They also give us a hell of a lot of obstacles in terms of dating, and I have to say there is kind of a thrill sneaking around. Call me crazy, but it feels like the pieces of the puzzle will just fall into place."

Knox rakes a hand through his hair and his eyes peer up at me. "Huh… I guess the Bluetop water really does something to your braincells."

"Except not for you. Haven't seen you in a good mood in months." I take a sip of my drink, and as my lips leave the rim of the glass, I realize I should move the focus off me. "You… how are you holding up?" My tone says enough. Knox was for sure close with our dad and maybe that still has him out of sorts.

"Nah, I'm good, if you think I'm in some depression or something. We had a year to be ready for it, and I don't regret anything from the past year. Dad lived his best life. Hell, he was drinking our wine until the very last day. He'll be waiting for us on the other side with poker cards ready and expecting us to have brought a bottle of our finest."

A subtle smile of acknowledgment graces my lips. "He

will. And he will be most excited to see you, and maybe Bennett," I joke with a little black humor.

Knox looks at me and huffs out a breath. "It's funny. You and him, just two men who respected each other and said nothing much more. But damn, he loved you in his own way, because of all the houses he could have bought to move him and Lucy to, he picked the one next to the love of your life. He either wanted to torture you or push you into the direction of lifetime happiness. I want to believe it's the latter, so do me a favor?"

Taking in his words, it causes me more emotion than I thought I was capable of in relation to this topic. I'm not unaffected, and truthfully, I've been riding on neutral on this topic since Dad passed. "What?" I ask.

"Get it right."

———

LYING on my back on her bed, Brooke sits on top of me wearing cute-as-fuck pajama shorts and a tank top. Those pastel-colored cotton pieces are my downfall. The fabric molds around her tits to perfection, and her nipples peak out like little treats. Her fingertips are firmly set on my stomach.

After helping Knox with a few odd jobs, I picked Lucy up, we had dinner, and then when she went to bed for the night, I snuck over like a man who can't be tamed.

We have lost time to make up for, and today I need her in my arms as a way of comfort.

"You okay? Your mind seems… somewhere else?" The concern in her voice is evident.

I interlace our hands and encourage her forward by pulling her arms until she's lying on top of me with her ear against my chest and her flowery-scented hair beneath my nose.

"Yeah, it's just something Knox said earlier... it got to me a little."

"Oh? What was that?"

I debate if I should tell her. It's not that it's a secret, but I don't want to bring a heavy undertone to our evening.

"Doesn't matter." Wrapping my arms around her, we tightly bind together, and I gaze down at her face, looking at me with equal parts hope and curiosity. "Can I ask you something?"

She answers instantly. "Of course."

"Did my dad ever talk about me with you? I mean, he was your neighbor."

A knowing smile arrives on her face. "He was respectful and didn't pry... on a regular basis. But, yeah, he had a thing for bringing up your name in the moments when hearing your name could send me into a tailspin. He just always knew when to do it."

"I caused a tailspin?"

"You know you did. Now let me show you how you've occupied my mind lately."

Oh, this woman, a little temptress.

"I completely approve of the demonstration about to happen."

It doesn't take long for my mind to focus on only one thing—Brooke coming undone on top of me. And yeah, she milks me dry too.

———

WHEN MY EYES BLINK OPEN, I realize we both fell asleep which, as much as I want to spend all night with her, is not logistically on the table quite yet.

Grabbing my phone from the side table, I see it's almost six in the morning. *Shit.*

Brooke murmurs in her sleep as I try not to wake her and untangle our limbs from one another.

As much as I need to speed up my departure, I can't help staring at her lying in bed naked. Perfectly content, unapologetically beautiful, most definitely not innocent—and my dick reacts to that thought.

Shaking my head as I sit up, I quickly grab my clothes, kiss her forehead, and make my escape by route choice B— the backdoor.

The morning spring air only wakens me halfway during the dusk-light thirty-second walk. It's only when I'm sliding open the backdoor of my own house and the smell of fresh coffee hits my nose that I wake to full alert.

My eyes dart to the coffee maker in the lit kitchen, and then my sight lands at the kitchen counter to Lucy sitting there with mug in hand and a smirk on her face.

"Sneaking in?" she asks in a tone that is pure I-caught-you-and-this-will-be-fun.

Do not let her get bargaining points from this. Do. Not.

I walk to the coffee pot. "What the hell are you doing up at this time? You are *never* up at this time."

"Calculus test first period, needed the extra study time," she quickly answers. "So, pretty positive this is possibly you setting the worst example for me. I mean, you didn't even text or tell me where you were going, and say what now? Did you spend the night with someone from the opposite sex?" She throws a hand over her mouth in theatrical shock.

Grabbing a mug, I dread the next few minutes. "I'm also a grown adult."

"Yeah," she draws it out. "*But* you are also responsible for a *very* impressionable teenager, so I don't know if this is the route you should be going down." Her eyes pretend to be searching her brain.

I laugh to myself at this start to the day. Turning to her, with caffeine now in my hand, I give her my warning glare.

"You are right. But since I control your bank account, phone bill, and set the rules, then I think we can let this one pass."

"Ouch. Throw that in. How about you take me shopping and then I never mention this to our brothers and we call it even?" She drinks from her mug like this is normal.

I nearly cave, but I have to state my feeling on this. "I don't negotiate with terrorists."

Lucy smiles and doesn't say anything as she looks at me. "So, you and Brooke are a thing again?"

I nod.

"That's cool. You know you don't need to sneak around because of me. Half of my class probably have more sex than you and she do."

That thought makes me cringe, and I don't even want to know which side Lucy sits on in that statistic.

Leaning over the counter with my mug in hand, I know I can speak to her like an adult. "We're not sneaking around because of you, but I should have told you. It's more, we have to be sensitive to Rosie. It's not time yet for her to wonder why I'm kissing her mommy."

"I get that. So would you say you got back together before or after the playhouse creation?"

I look at her with caution. "Why do you ask?"

"Oh, nothing. I mean, if you were to give it a date, though, it would have been last Saturday?"

"Oh God, tell me you didn't."

Her face falls. "Bennett, Knox, and I may have had a bet."

I shake my head, not at all surprised.

"This family and this town really are unbelievable." Yet I can only smile. "Okay, what do you want for breakfast? Pancakes? Eggs? Hit Sally-Anne's for a full breakfast before school? We're both up."

"Can I drive us to Sally-Anne's?" Always negotiating.

"Sure."

Lucy now smiles in accomplishment and hops off the stool. "Awesome. Oh, and does this mean I have like a full-time babysitting gig since you want to date our neighbor with a kid?"

I cluck the inside of my cheek. "As a matter of fact, I need your babysitting services this weekend so I can take Brooke on a real date."

"Okay, but I'm upping my hourly rate if you don't return before midnight."

"Fine. Now give me five minutes to change and I'll meet you in the car—with the engine off." I point my finger to her.

"Deal."

As she heads to collect her things and I go to my room to change my shirt at least, my mind does a run-through of all my romantic date options because I need to knock this out of the park.

BROOKE

My phone vibrates on the kitchen counter as I stir the pot of mac 'n cheese. Glancing at the screen, I smile, seeing it's Grayson. The last few days have been a constant back and forth about how our days are going, what Rosie is up to, and how Lucy can rip him to pieces with a stare right before giving a hug of affection goodnight.

GRAYSON

Grayson: I'm picking you up in 10!

10 what?

Minutes, I'm taking you out.

A silent smile forms on my lips.

Except Rosie is here, about to snap from hunger.

I include an emoji of a devil and a unicorn.

Don't worry about it. Lucy is coming over now to take over the reins. Bonus points, she isn't even grounded...she volunteered!

He includes a shocked emoji.

I look down at my body and see that I may need a miracle to whip myself up in ten minutes. I have cheese powder on my t-shirt, the bun on my head has fallen flat, not to mention I have my not-for-Grayson's-eyes panties on.

Lucy greets me as she opens the front door. Just in time, I need every second I can get.

"Hey, Lucy. Are you sure?" I double-check as I'm already stepping back from the stove, excited for this surprise.

Lucy laughs silently to herself, and in that moment, I notice how her eyes have a similar glint to her brother's. She's a Blisswood alright.

"I have a history report due on Monday so it's not like I have other plans," she says, rubbing Rosie's hair, as Rosie is lost in her cartoons.

"Okay. Uhm, well, I guess watch the stove?" I begin to sprint to my room but stop and pivot my attention to Lucy. "Any clues for me?"

She shrugs. "I am not allowed to say, but I must say that he has his A-game on."

Oh geez, no pressure or anything.

Running to my room, I whip off my clothes in the process. Rummaging through my dresser drawer, I pull out a thong and quickly get it on before running to my closet and opting for a casual black dress that goes to my knees. I literally slide it on as I make my way to the bathroom. I have a young child, so getting makeup on in no time is a skill I've mastered. And since I like a challenge, I do my best to give myself a blowout with the hair dryer in two minutes.

By the time I'm looking in the mirror, satisfied with my outfit, simple jewelry, a dash of perfume, and a jean jacket, then it hits me... I am going on a date.

Walking back into the living room, Lucy whistles, and my daughter looks up at me.

"You so pretty, Mommy. Where are you going?" Rosie asks.

"Oh, uh, Mommy is..." I forgot what my cover story is. It shouldn't be difficult, she's three. For some reason I look to Lucy for help.

"Your mommy is going for a neighbor meeting with my brother."

Even my daughter looks between us, not entirely convinced.

I throw on an overdone smile. "Yep, neighbor meeting. Need to discuss... the tree between our houses."

Rosie makes a little noise of doubt before looking at the television then back at me. "Okay, Mommy."

Relief hits me as I nod goodbye to Lucy and head outside. I don't notice Grayson anywhere which is odd, as he said ten minutes, and when I look at my phone, I see that I am actually three minutes late, so I text him.

> Outside but where are you?

> Around the corner, like the good old times.

I try to keep my beaming smile in check as I nearly skip around the block to find Grayson Blisswood leaning against his car like a man from a 1950s commercial. No, even better, like a nineties Dylan from *90210,* complete with the early-evening sun shining on his face.

"We're doing this again? This is the ultimate throwback to when I was seventeen," I say as I walk into his arms, and he greets me with a warm, slow agonizing kiss that is a hint of the night ahead.

"The stakes are completely different. Your parents totally knew what was going down between us every time and never once gave us a lecture. Princess Rosie, on the other hand… yikes, the kid may throw some playdough in my direction before she sweet-talks me into that princess pony tea party she wants to have." His fingertips glide down my cheek as he stares at my lips.

The other day, he came over for a coffee when Rosie came back from school and played for an hour at the kitchen table. I'm still finding droplets of fluorescent orange dough around the kitchen.

"You couldn't give me more notice about this impromptu date? I mean, what is this?" I give him a sheepish grin.

His arm comes around my shoulders as he walks me to the passenger side of the car.

"You and I are not just going to be fuck buddies. And yes, I noticed the pattern we were getting ourselves into." His eyes peer down at me all knowingly, and he's right. We haven't done much outside of my bedroom. "We're way more than that, so let's go on a real date. The kind that has us both kind of nervous and waiting for me to kiss you at the end of the night. But spoiler alert, I'm going to kiss you between every damn dinner course, because with our history, we get to skip a few steps."

He holds the car door open for me as I slide onto the seat, loving all of his romantic words.

———

WE'RE SITTING in the corner of the restaurant overlooking the state park and fords. On the way down, we drove along the Rock River where a river boat moved down the water.

I smile, as Grayson decided to drive us a good thirty or so miles away from Bluetop. There are only so many spots in town, and even fewer without an audience. But the drive alone was slightly breathtaking, with bison over the grasslands, the nature parks along the Chicago-Iowa trail, and the man I can call my own holding my hand while he drove.

He thanks the waiter for bringing our glasses of wine. Even though Olive Owl has a bottle on the menu, he opted for a bottle from another Illinois winery near the Mississippi River not far from here.

"Hey, didn't you take me here once?" I know why this is all familiar.

"I did." He smirks to himself as he closes his menu. "The summer before I left for college. Maybe... I don't know. I wanted that summer to be good for us. Saved up for it, but in the end my father slipped me a bunch of cash to take you out." A fondness flashes across his face before he blinks and opens his eyes in my direction. "Times have changed. Now I could buy this place out."

I rest my hand on top of his on the table. "It is different this time, and in that spirit..." My other hand grabs my wine, and he follows my actions as I tilt my glass to his. "As much as our memories are a part of us, you can't relive memories no matter how hard we try. We definitely can skip a few of the early stages of a relationship. But Grays, you and me, it's a completely new chapter. This is us now, okay?" I need him to understand that we are starting fresh.

"I know," he promises. "Now let's toast the hell out of the start of this chapter."

Ah, that grin. My panties have already reached their demise. The third pair this week.

Alas, I stay focused on this poignant scene in front of me.

Our glasses touch. "We're going to get this right, Grayson."

"We will. This chapter and our next."

I smile in approval before the clink of our glasses fills our table and we both drink our red wine.

When the waiter returns to take our orders, Grayson indicates to give us a minute, and our eyes stay glued on each other. Hell, there could be a fire and we would be oblivious.

How is it possible to feel so reunited when we've barely gotten started? I mean, yeah, we have daily contact. And he has felt every inch of me too, but we haven't had many opportunities just me and him without the pressure of time.

"Surprise me, Grayson, tell me anything." I bring my hand to prop my chin up as I lean into the table and admire the man in front of me.

"I feel like Chicago was another lifetime ago, even though it was only a few months. Work phoned me yesterday with an opportunity—two, actually."

My stomach is already twisting with pain. Ambition and Grayson together never ends well for me. He must sense my fear, and he places his hand on my thigh.

"To design a new library down in Austin, I could even lead the project."

I swallow and I feel unable to move.

"I said no. My sister kind of needs me around and so does my neighbor—or rather, I need her around." He tips his head to the side.

He glances up as the waiter drops a bread roll basket on the table, which only prolongs the second part of his sentence.

"The other opportunity?" I ask.

"Nothing big league, not for sure, but maybe they'll consider me for a project up near Madison. That's a doable commute a few times a month."

On a good day, it can be done in an hour-and-a-half drive.

"That's something. I'll keep my fingers crossed for you… but you talking about work isn't a surprise," I have to remind him.

"Fair point. How about… I think I may help Coach out, just a few times."

"That's kind of funny. And it *does* surprise me. Volunteering yourself to hang around with more teenagers? But I bet they will love it. I may casually take Rosie to the playground near the field and check out the coaching goods." I wiggle my eyebrows at him.

"Don't do that. I may feel the need to impress, and I'm not sure I even have it in me to slide into home base."

I chortle at his sentence because it opens the door for so many jokes. "Trust me, you have managed just fine."

He shakes his head, entertained.

I grab a roll because my stomach is growling. The moment I begin to butter my roll, he looks at me with wide eyes. "Ah," he says, "still doing the first-date polite lathering of butter on your bread when I am confident you want the whole thing smothered in the honey butter they provide. It's okay, you can let loose around me, I've seen your wild side." He even winks at me.

I'm soon in stiches of laughter, and so it goes for the rest of the evening. We taste each other's food, we order dessert, and he moves his chair closer to me as the night progresses.

"Maybe one day I'll go back into ER nursing, but for now it works with Rosie, and I'm okay with that. I can't imagine life without her or what it would even look like. Ask me again in ten years when she's not so dependent on me," I honestly answer when he asked me about work.

"As long as you're happy, B, and we already know Rosie is content as can be."

"I like to think so. Anyhow, I just wish she had more family around. My parents visit a few times a year, but it's not the same." I glance up as the waiter places two plates of dessert down. Death-by-chocolate cake and raspberry pie with vanilla ice cream.

We thank the college-aged man and quickly grab our spoons. "Well, I'm saving up for a place for me and Rosie. Although my parents don't live at their house anymore, eventually they'll sell, then I want to find a place for us."

"In Bluetop," he double-checks.

"Yeah, it's all she knows. It's home for me too. I can't imagine life away from here. Maybe I should have been more adventurous. It's not that I'm afraid of living anywhere else, it's just that I'm comfortable with the familiar."

The corner of his mouth tugs at my answer. "I know. Sometimes we need to step out of our comfort zones, then if it leads you back to where you left, it's meant to be."

My head perks up from his words. "Is that what you believe?"

"I'm beginning to," he answers simply.

It's hopeful to say the least, and I don't hear regret either. The taste of pie hitting my tongue causes me to moan, and Grayson looks at me peculiarly.

"I really wish I could master a raspberry pie recipe," I mention as I dive my spoon in.

"Your baking threw off all the moms at the bake sale, but Lucy doesn't have it in her to lie, so you got all the credit for the cookie save," he promises.

I smile as I swallow. "Were you planning on passing off

my cookies as your own? Isn't that like a form of plagiarism?"

"Trust me, I would make it up to you in full, with interest."

"I know you would." I like the imagery floating in my head.

He guides the spoon of chocolate cake in my direction, and I take it into my mouth. Also, a good contender on the food front.

"Next date you pick our destination," he says.

I bring a finger to my chin as I think about the options. "Maybe a hike or picnic. We are still in shape... enough."

"Sounds good. We can drive to Lake Galena or up to Lake Geneva."

"You keep giving suggestions away from Bluetop. Eventually, we are going to have to cave. I'm positive Mr. Bigsly already saw us manhandling one another on the street corner. Won't take long for Sally-Anne to figure out your Saturday order of extra muffins is for us, and oh my, Helen can't stop smiling at me like a Cheshire cat when I run into her at the grocery store. We're screwed."

Grayson leans back in his chair more in defeat from the dessert than anything else. "I'm trying to respect the whole going-slow thing."

I play with my fork on the plate. "Thank you, I can see you are fully committed to the slow cause."

"For you, anything."

I nod in understanding, and once again we get a little lost in the moment, until he breaks it.

"Shall I pay the bill and we'll head back?"

"Sounds good."

As he settles the bill and I freshen up in the restroom, I look in the mirror. The same one that saw me when I was seventeen, with my boyfriend about to head off to college. And now in the mirror I see myself as a single mom who I think has it together. It's still me, but as silly as it sounds, I have more direction now, and the crazy thing is, I think Grayson does too.

Making my way to the doors, Grayson is waiting for me by the entrance, and he interlaces our hands. I can smell the mint he must have popped into his mouth. It's a nice combination with his cologne, and it delivers the message that he is certain what direction he wants to go with our night ahead.

"Want to go for a little walk?"

I scoff a laugh at the mere suggestion. "It's nighttime, and I am positive this is raccoon territory."

"And? I'm sure my strong arms can protect you."

"Skunks? Possums?"

His face scrunches, and he leads us away. "Good point. Drive back it is."

But I stop him, step closer, and plant a hard kiss on his lips. I've had a lovely evening, a *great* evening, and it's with him. That deserves a proving kiss. A confirmation that we are together, and his fuck-buddy theory is nowhere on the radar. His hands comb through my hair as he holds me firmly in place, and we both murmur sounds that I'm sure the wildlife will mistake as a mating call.

I can't get enough of him, and he knows it, which is why he grumbles when he pulls away. I smile at succeeding to leave him breathless. "How about we stop somewhere on the way back?" I lean in to whisper in his ear in a sultry tone. "We should revisit the backseat scenario."

He groans as he steps away. "I'm not sure we're going to make it out of the parking lot." He yanks my hand and I follow him to the car.

We make it 1.7 miles, to be exact.

16

GRAYSON

The teenage boys stare at me with a bewildered look, sweat running down their faces as Coach Dingle still knows how to run a brutal session. Standing there with my hands on my hips, sporting a Bluetop High t-shirt—since I like to take it a step too far on the all-in front—the boys are wondering what I have in store for them.

"Okay, boys, everyone warmed up?" Coach grabs the whistle from around his neck in preparation.

"You made us run twenty laps, so yeah… we're warmed up," one of the boys gives us his mundane-toned answer.

Coach glances at me with a knowing smirk.

"What's the golden boy doing here?" another guy pipes up.

I'm still asking myself that question, but what the hell. I'm ahead on designs, completely enamored with Brooke, and Coach won't give up until I make an appearance.

"Grayson was an all-star player for our team, and you met him at the BBQ the other day. I've asked him to help with throwing the ball and mitt catching."

"I'll go easy," I promise with a smile.

Coach blows the whistle, and the boys divide into pairs. It doesn't take long for me to eye who needs the most help, so I jog a few feet in their direction. Pulling the mitt from the back of my jeans, I quickly show the scrawny kid how to hold the glove up in front of his body in a better position.

Watching the two for a few throws, I pat his back before heading to the next pair. The team is good—well, maybe seventy percent good. They all seem so… young. Or I've just aged *a lot.*

Once the team is underway, I walk to Coach who is scribbling notes on his tablet. Scanning the field, I notice the track team still running, cheerleaders practicing a pyramid, and a group of what I'll say look like gothic-inspired teenagers sketching on pads of paper in the stands.

Lucy said she needed to study in the library for a test, which is all the more reason why I'm surprised to spot her in the corner of my eye talking to some guy who in no way looks to be her age in the parking lot. I think I've noticed him once before too and they were talking. Oh yeah, the guy who made me temporarily change my party policy.

"I take it he isn't into team sports," I state, with eyes fixed on my accidental spying target.

Coach looks and returns to focusing on his tablet. "He isn't even a student."

My fists now flex at my sides and my jaw tightens.

A humorous sound escapes from Coach. "Relax. Drew wouldn't hurt a soul, even though he is quite a good boxer."

I turn my attention to Coach and lift my sunglasses to my head. "He has a name."

Coach tucks the tablet under his arm. "Of course he does, we all do. He graduated a year ago."

My eyes grow wild, I feel it. "You're not helping my imagination right now, Coach."

"Drew sometimes helps out around the school. He hasn't had the best of lives, and we all deserve a break."

Turning my gaze away for a second, I look at the man who trained me for four years straight and wrote me a heart-felt condolence letter when my dad passed. "Sure, but not with my sister."

He holds a hand up to pause me. "He wouldn't dare. I'm sure they're just chatting. Go easy on him. He could use a role model, never really got that much from anyone."

"I'll think about it, but right now I'm not thinking too clearly."

"Run it off."

I look at the older man, surprised, and see he isn't even joking.

"One lap will clear your head," he assures me.

My gaze shoots between him and my sister in the parking lot talking with the kid who pretty much looks like an edgy guy with too many muscles. It's a reminder of Knox at that age, and that isn't reassuring.

Ugh. I want to run right into her direction.

But then I see her wave him off and I calm down slightly and decide to run half a lap.

————

"You can help me with my Spanish test prep, right?" Lucy asks as she scrolls through her phone in the front seat.

"I can try." I'm driving us back home, and I haven't said much, as she seems occupied. "Hey, Lucy, that guy you were talking to earlier…"

She smiles to herself. "Drew? It's nothing, so no need to go into some weird brother-bear transformation."

I glance quickly to her before I focus my attention on the rearview mirror.

"It's not that you can't have a boyfriend, but he is a lot older than you. What, nineteen?"

Lucy grumbles. "Can we stop this convo now? Really not needed."

"Fine. Just know that I wouldn't approve."

"Wouldn't be asking for approval even if interested," she reminds me, full of sass, and it causes me to smirk to myself.

"Great convo." I throw a little fist pump into the sky, and it makes her roll her eyes with a huff.

She throws her AirPods in which tells me that I'm in the doghouse for a little bit.

I take this opportunity of silence to call Brooke on my Bluetooth. After two rings she picks up.

"Hey there." She sounds bubbly and in a good mood.

"Hey, I'm on my way back home with Lucy. How's Rosie today? Any hot dates tonight?"

"Me or Rosie?"

I guess I didn't phrase my sentence right. "Both."

"Nothing much. Any hot offers?"

Then it dawns on me that I'm hungry and probably everyone else is too.

"What about a good-looking pizza delivery guy and his cheeky sister?"

"Depends if he has pineapple on that pizza and throws in breadsticks for a bonus."

"Damn, if I'm getting a bonus then I'll throw in chicken wings too."

My sister turns her head to me and takes an earbud out. "You two really need to dial back this cutesy thing. I literally just lost my appetite."

"Oh, sorry," Brooke quickly apologizes on the end of the line.

"It's fine," Lucy says. "I guess I translate this conversation to we are having pizza for dinner?"

"Yep," I confirm.

Forty-five minutes later, Lucy and I are walking into Brooke's kitchen with boxes of food in our hands, and Rosie is jumping up and down since pizza is one of her magic words.

"Cheese! We have cheese!" Rosie's tone squeals.

"I think there is cheese, but you need to go wash your hands first." Brooke places her hands on Rosie's shoulders where she's standing behind her.

"Come on, squirt, I need the bathroom anyways." Lucy offers her hand to Rosie, and they walk together.

It leaves Brooke and me alone, and I intend to take full advantage of the moment.

Grabbing Brooke's wrist, I wind her to me until she lands against my chest. Leaning down, I capture her mouth, to which she tilts her head up to grant me the only kind of welcome I like. Her lips taste sweet, as if she had bubble gum earlier. The raspy little noises she makes encourages me to take more.

It's only when her hand presses against my chest that I begin to part, realizing we're moving too fast.

"Easy there," she whispers.

"I need to take all I can get. I'm on Spanish-tutor duty tonight, so I'm not sure I can sneak over."

"You speak Spanish?" Her expression turns puzzled.

"Barely, but I'm sure the app and I can master high school Spanish. I promised Lucy, and I've already annoyed her enough today." I rub a hand across my forehead.

Brooke touches my chest affectionately. "Wasn't a fan of you hanging around her school?"

"No, not a fan of me spying on her, more like it."

She brings a finger up and swerves it side to side. "That's a no-no."

I step to her because that whole move was an image of an enticing invite, and I want her to use that pouty tone before I slam into her and show her how much she could enjoy a little disobedience.

Brooke grins and her eyes narrow. "You're having a dirty thought. I know it."

"I promise it is ten times dirtier than what you're thinking." I dive in to tease her neck, causing her head to fall back. I glide my lips along her skin and nip a few times before returning to her mouth that I demolish with my own.

She hums and speaks against my lips as she twists the fabric of my t-shirt around her fist. "This outfit of yours mixed with sweat is so fucking good."

"Language, Brooke," I taunt her while I trap her between me and the counter. We forget to breathe... or think.

"What are you doing to my mommy?"

Brooke and I freeze and our eyes dart to the side as our lips slowly pull apart.

Lucy tried to blind Rosie's eyes with her hand. "Smooth, real smooth," she scolds us.

Stepping apart, Brooke quickly straightens her shirt then runs to Rosie and leans down. "Grays was…"

"This is going to be good," Lucy mumbles, and I give her the death stare.

Brooke bites her bottom lip as she looks at me then back to Rosie and takes a grip of her little arms.

"You were kissing," Rosie simply states, slightly confused.

"Yeah, yeah, we were," Brooke answers. "The thing is… Grayson and I are together."

I don't know if this is where I jump in or if I stay mute. This is officially a first for me, and in all honesty, it's slightly more petrifying than meeting the parents or talking about a future.

Rosie blinks, still not grasping what it means.

"Like, more than friends," Brooke continues and waits patiently. "As in my… boyfriend," she nearly slurs out.

Rosie shoots her stare at me then back to Brooke. "Oh, okay." She walks to the chair at the island and climbs up the stool to look at the pizza on the counter.

Brooke shrugs to me and seems confused that Rosie is so at ease.

"You okay, kiddo?" I ask. "With your mom and me?" I slide into the stool across from her.

"Sure. You made me a playhouse."

I grin at her association. "That's it?"

"Can you scare monsters away?"

"I think I can do that. Why?"

"Because sometimes I hear one at night. He goes to Mommy's room."

My head falls into my hand as I hear Lucy and Brooke trying not to burst into hysterics.

The monster is me, totally me. I tripped over a Mr. Potato Head the other night on my way sneaking out.

"I think I can, uh, take care of that, no problem. I know the monster quite well, we're on good terms," I promise.

This was too easy, and even I know that it's never that simple.

17

BROOKE

My freshly polished baby-blue nails on the steering wheel make me smile, as it matches everything I'm wearing—including what's on underneath. Tonight, it's date night and not the kind where we have a curfew. The whole night and morning are ours, thanks to Kelsey watching Rosie and Lucy having a sleepover at a friend's.

I have it all planned, from trying a new stir-fry recipe down to what I will be wearing the moment Grays comes through the door. He's at Olive Owl all day to help his brothers, and I'm sure he will bring a few bottles of wine back for us.

The last two weeks since Rosie found out we were dating, we have done a lot of things together, Grayson, me, and the girls. Grayson's taken Rosie a few times to Olive Owl too, as Lucy's horse Cosmo is there. The picnic was probably my favorite highlight of the week; Rosie spent most of the time feeding Grayson grapes while I admired the scene in front of me.

The sound system of the car indicates that I have an

incoming call, and the moment I see Grayson's name flash across the screen, I press okay on my steering wheel.

"Change of plans."

"Hello to you too." I smile as I wait patiently for the traffic light to turn green.

"Sorry, I don't have long. How about you meet me here at Olive Owl instead of your place later? We had a cancellation, so a very romantic room that we once occupied is free and calling our name."

Wow, that is an excellent change of plan. I would have messed up the spices in the stir fry anyhow. "Oh? Well, I guess I can save my idea of you arriving home to find me cooking at the stove in your high school jersey for another day," I play coy.

The delicious groan that comes through the phone is the type that makes heat coil between my legs.

"Fuck, now I have a hard situation to take care of. But am I allowed a raincheck for that scenario?" I can imagine him scanning the area to ensure nobody spots his impressive bulge.

"Absolutely. Can't wait for later... Wait, do you mean *the* room?"

"Yep. Fate, huh? See you later, beautiful."

When our call ends, I smile to myself that this date night just got upgraded to a special occasion. Or it feels that way. The logistical change sends me into a blissful state where time seems to stop.

Because by the time I arrive to my house to now pack a bag, I only notice the man standing outside my front door after I've parked my car.

The moment I open the car door, every feeling of contentment zooms out and disperses to a distant memory.

My heart and stomach sink as my eyes confirm that

Adam, Rosie's biological dad, is standing outside my front door.

I haven't seen him or had contact with him in four years. He looks the same, maybe a little more bulky in terms of muscle, but his short spiky brown hair and dark eyes are the same. He gives me a gentle nod when I ascend the path to the front door.

"Hey, Brooke." He says it casually, as if this isn't odd at all.

"Wh-what are you doing here, Adam?" I stagger out, confused, and my mind goes blank.

"Can we talk?"

I reluctantly answer and blink a few times to make sure that I'm not imagining things. "Oh... I'm not really sure what you're doing here. We haven't spoken in four years." A nervous laugh escapes me and surprises me too, because fear is making its way up my veins.

He would never hurt me. He's a decent guy, and even though he wanted no part in raising Rosie, he has always been honest and that's what he delivered. I gave him an out and he took it, and that's fine.

But something about this situation has me on edge.

Adam places his hands in his jeans pockets. "I know, but it's important."

"Okay, we can, I guess, talk out here." Because I am definitely not letting him in; I don't want him to see Rosie's things.

I sit on the bench swing as Adam finds a spot on the wicker stool on the other side of the porch.

"This isn't easy, but I'm engaged, and we're trying to have a baby," he begins.

Geez, now suddenly he wants to try being a father to a child. Should have done that four years ago when he said he had a firm no-kid policy, that he never wanted to be a father.

I bite my tongue to stop myself from speaking and it causes my cheeks to tighten. Instead, I offer a short, "And?"

"We are having trouble conceiving, and when we did all the tests, we discovered that, well..." He looks to me and something that looks like embarrassment spreads across his face. "It's me who has the issue."

"Again, and?" I'm not processing anything, as I'm still surprised he's here.

He brings his hands together and huffs out a breath. "We don't know when my, well, count went to almost non-existent, but it's unlikely that I'm able to get someone... pregnant." He waits for the pin to drop.

But it isn't something so tiny as a pin dropping, it's a thousand pieces of glass. A metallic taste hits my tongue because I bite it so hard. I hear a buzzing in my ears, and I sit there frozen. "Are you're saying that Rosie isn't yours?" I need to hear another confirmation of something I've always wished for.

Rosie is Grayson's.

"This isn't happening," I mumble to myself.

Adam waits a moment before continuing. "The thing is, since we don't know if I've always been this way, then if Rosie is mine..."

Fear grows inside of me, and I don't like where this conversation is going.

"Don't say it." I shake my head and grip the ends of my sleeves out of nervous habit.

"She could be my only biological child, my only chance, and I don't want to miss out on that."

"You signed away your rights," I bluntly remind him, and internally, the panic multiplies.

"I know, but maybe we can explore options." He's calm and doesn't sound vindictive, instead almost sensitive, as if he's walking on eggshells around me.

I feel like I am about to fall into pieces, and this man clearly thinks he's being noble, but he is presenting me with facts that only make my wishful theory more possible.

Grayson is Rosie's father.

Swallowing, I feel the need to throw up, and I do my best to calm it with a few breaths. I have no choice but to be strong in this position. "Can we first figure out if Rosie is yours?"

"Of course."

A long silence overtakes us, and to be honest, it feels as though the world swallowed us all whole and Grayson doesn't even know he's sinking yet.

"I'm sorry to show up like this. I've been trying to contact you. I had my lawyer send a letter about three months ago, and then when we got no answer, I emailed you."

"I blocked you. Must have gone to spam," I answer simply. I rub my temples with my fingers as I try and process everything. "Wait, what do you mean you sent a letter?"

"You clearly never got it. My lawyer delivered it in person to your father."

My body straightens to full attention. "My father hasn't been here since Thanksgiving, it wouldn't have been him."

"My lawyer said the man was out in the yard and looked a little sick and signed for it as your father."

I hold a hand out, still confused. "Really, the only man around here my father's age was my next-door neighbor, but he passed around two months ago—"

Shaking my head, I laugh to myself almost hysterically. My eyes glare as I realize yet another twist to this day.

Grayson's father.

He knew.

He took the letter with the information that I would have wanted to know, Grayson would have wanted to know. The clue that makes it appear that Rosie is most likely his grand-daughter. He carried the secret to his grave.

A special night this is going to be.

18

GRAYSON

I walk with my brothers as we clean up the mess left by a group who were in for a wine tasting. It's our fifth this season, and we're just getting started. Glancing around, I take in the perfect lighting, a deep warm hue, the fireplace crackling low, and the remnants of cheese and bottles with a few droplets of wine left sitting on the tables.

Bennett looks on proudly as he grabs another bottle. "A good crowd today. I like when they're around our age and know how to have a good—and responsible—time."

"You and Knox really have the Olive Owl history down," I say. "Fifty percent believable and fifty percent bull, and Christ, stop flashing those looks at the women. We're going to get a reputation and not for our farm products." I let them lead the way on these things, and I only help answer questions or help pour wine when they're short on hands.

"Maybe Knox and I are the selling point, we should use our charm," he answers with pride.

As I stack a few plates together, I look at my watch.

"Big plans?" Bennett asks with the corner of his mouth

curving up. "Anything to do with the cancellation we had on one of the rooms in the bed-and-breakfast?"

I shoot my finger out at him. "Bingo."

Life is easier when we're not sneaking around. I love having the side commentary of a teenager and preschooler, but being chaperoned every date isn't for the faint of heart. It's an express train to blue-balls territory.

Now, my girlfriend and I are finally able to have a full night together, and even better, the opportunity presented itself.

"We will be taking full advantage of that room," I confirm, and I already know the grin on my face couldn't be scrubbed off if anyone tried.

"Good for you. It's nice to see it's working out."

Under Bennett's muscly exterior, he is a giant teddy bear most of the time. He's entirely genuine with every word he says.

"I mean, I assume nobody else needs the room?" I've been trying to figure out what Bennett has been up to, because no man is as calm as he is without having someone to entangle with, and he isn't dropping any hints either.

He crosses his arms and leans against the bar. "Nah, I'm more a roll-in-the-hay kind of guy. You're fine, but breakfast isn't included," he teases me.

"Deal." The moment I say that I spot Brooke arriving with a small bag over her shoulder, hair down and a cute-as-fuck blue dress that matches those baby blues I love so much. She wiggles her fingers at my brother, but I can't help noticing that her usual pleasant smile isn't what she is feeling, I know her too well.

"Hey, it looks good here," she greets Bennett.

"Not looking too bad yourself." He tilts his head in approval.

"Breathtaking, actually," I add, and her blush spreading across her face, mixed with her bold eyes, seems to be tinged with a sadness that I don't quite understand. Yet still she's beautiful.

Bennett clears his throat. "Well, you two kids keep it safe." He offers us a little wave with two fingers before heading off to the kitchen.

He leaves Brooke and me alone. Instantly I grab her bag to be a gentleman, although I have no intention of maintaining that facade.

"Here we are again," she husks as her eyes glitter with intent.

"I think we can skip the tour this time."

"What if that was the best part?" she dares me, slightly weakly, with an arched brow.

I laugh under my breath at the mere notion of it.

Offering her my hand, the moment her skin touches my own it all comes back.

As if every step is a reminder of what led us to each other's arms last time—it didn't take many steps.

My heart picks up into a thrumming beat, her lips part, and her breath sounds heavy.

The entire journey upstairs is our own personal silent trip down memory lane.

Arriving to the very room we had our night together, I open the door and we walk in. The moment the door closes, she glances over her shoulder at me with an almost sly grin. Her fingers hook under the straps of her dress before quickly pulling them down to her hips to reveal she has matching baby-blue lingerie, and it's lacy.

I can't believe my eyes, and I drop her bag in one giant thump. "You are full of surprises."

Stepping to her, I wrap my arms around her from behind

and inhale her fruity scent; I'm still positive it's watermelon and have never checked because it could be any fruit under the sun for all I care.

I glance around the room. It's smaller compared to the others, but people like the romantic appeal, down to the white lace quilt and high-thread-count sheets. Plus, it's our room, our place.

"We have all night," I murmur into her hair, and I feel her breath quicken.

"Is that a reminder or a warning?" She's toying with me in that sultry voice.

Tonight can be slow and everything we would hope it to be, but I am not going to hold off on touching her or making her beg.

"Definitely a warning," I quickly answer before our mouths meet for a kiss that sinks us into the moment, with the world around us going still.

But it doesn't fade, the thought that she is slightly off. Caressing her cheek with the back of my hand, I ask, "Everything okay? You seem a little… in another world."

Subtly she shakes her head in agreement and takes my hands in hers. "There is something, but right now I just want this, us. Can we have that? We'll talk after. Can you do that for me?"

Studying her, I know now that she is seeking comfort or a momentary escape from whatever is on her mind. I should question it more, but I want to give her what she needs, and I sense an urgency in her to help her not fall apart. I'll keep her safe in my arms.

Kissing her forehead, I promise, "Tonight's just us."

Relief floods her eyes, and I begin us on our journey.

My hands roam lower and wildly. My left hand caresses

the curve of her ass and the other rides up her soft thigh, catching between her skin and the fabric.

Peering down, I see her hard nipples peek through the fabric, and it's the signal to my cock to explore her body until she is writhing under me.

Kissing down her neck and chest, I slither lower until I am on my knees before her.

"You know how beautiful you are?" I whisper. I want to worship this body that I'm holding.

I got to be her first, her middle, and I hope to be her last.

Still, even after all these years, her body is something else. Her curves are better, tits perkier, and she still has an influence on me that is unexplainable with time.

"Grayson," she whispers because she gets shy with praise.

I slide her thong off so all I have to do is shimmy her little dress number up her body, and I don't waste time as I grip her hips to steady her, and my tongue licks her slit, causing her to gasp.

Finding a pattern that has her repeatedly moaning, I don't relent. I need her to come on my tongue, I need her undone.

"You're not giving me much chance to take this slow or take care of you," she breathlessly says as her hands plant on my shoulders so she doesn't fall.

I keep going, and just when I think I am about to take her to her first release, she urges me up. I obey, but not for long. The moment I stand, I pick her up and walk us to the bed where I drop her on the mattress and quickly come to hover over her body.

Her legs part wide, inviting me to settle between them as we kiss, and her hands yank at my clothing.

"What if I tell you that I'm going to take you many ways tonight?"

"Sounds like I won't be walking normal tomorrow," Brooke quips.

I move her leg as high as it can go—it's far. She is still far too flexible for the imagination. My cock responds by twitching, and even in my boxer briefs, pressing into her pussy feels like a step toward heaven.

Kissing down to her inner thigh, I debate where to begin. "These legs will be wrapped around my neck a lot tonight."

"Oh yeah?" She arches her chest up as she settles on the mattress and her hands mold to caress her breasts and tease me.

"Yeah, and I'll come over your tits too."

My words make her pelvis tilt up to me; she likes what's coming out of my mouth.

"Do I get to have you in my mouth?"

I reach up and grab her jaw gently. "Yes, we'll do it all. You're mine, you know that, right?"

She licks her lips. "Take me, Grayson," she insists, with her eyes showing me she's waiting.

"Not until you and I are completely naked, and you tell me you're mine."

She squirms underneath me, and I move to lean on my side, watching her as she removes the lingerie until she's lying before me naked against the mattress. Her fingers reach out to indicate that I need to lose my boxer briefs.

It doesn't take long until we're lying next to one another, naked and staring into each other's eyes. I roll us so she's beneath me, and I dip my head down so we can kiss firmly.

"I'm yours, so take what is yours," she whispers, and the feeling of her hand stroking my cock as I kiss her deeply is perfection—almost.

Pinning one of her wrists to the bed, I remind her of a

fact. "I don't need to take it, as you're already mine. Always have been."

With our foreheads touching, I enter her slowly, waiting for her cue to go deeper. Now this... this is perfection. Her heat wrapping around my cock as her eyes stay locked with mine.

Together as one.

I know I've missed this; I was a fool to try and live without this feeling. It's all her, my one and only.

Lifting her legs again, the new angle causes us both to groan in pleasure.

I reach down for a quick kiss before continuing my quest to get us both to orgasm.

"Always," she says drowsily as her eyes hood closed.

————

BROOKE KISSES my chest to wake me, and when our eyes catch, she attempts a smile.

"This isn't a bad way to wake up," I note as I try to wake to full attention, but my cock is already a few steps ahead of me. I mentally rein him in and instead opt to pull Brooke closer. Maybe a late morning sleep-in is in our cards.

But a few minutes later and I sense she's still not making any attempt to rest. Lifting one eye open, I see she has been staring at me with her chin resting on her hands splayed across my chest.

I've noticed a few times in the last few weeks that sometimes she seems lost in thought as her eyes don't leave me. As much as I would love to say that it's from admiration, I'm not going to let my ego take the credit. Something is going on in her head. She indicated as much last night, and now it's time to address it.

"Yes?" I draw out the question.

Brooke bites her bottom lip as she contemplates what to say. "Just noticing the way your lips twitch when your eyes are closed. It's… familiar."

Both my eyes open at her odd observation. "Not sure it's changed over the years."

"You're right, it's just…"

Okay, now she's acting weird, and I shuffle my body until I'm sitting up and leaning against the headboard—the one we nearly broke last night.

"Now it's time to talk. Everything okay?" I touch both of her shoulders, ready to qualm any doubts that she may be having.

She looks away then back at me. "Yeah." That was very unconvincing. "Uhm, well, no. Maybe?"

Sliding out of bed, I search for clothes. "Now you have me freaking out slightly. Should I be worried?"

Brooke stays sitting up in bed with the sheet wrapped around her. Panic seems to be flooding her face as her chest begins to move rapidly. Her focus is burning her gaze into the mattress. Until she looks up at me.

"Rosie. What if she's really yours?"

My world literally stops.

19

BROOKE

Grayson looks at me with his jaw tightened and eyes ablaze, letting my words sink in.

My doubt. My hope. My secret. A confession.

I've always wondered if the chance the doctor got the date wrong was simply that… a possibility.

But the more I see Rosie and Grayson together, the more I feel like that my suspicion isn't so crazy. Then Adam's news just cemented it.

"What do you mean?" His tone is full of confusion.

I know I need to explain quickly if I ever have a hope of him not hating me.

Springing out of the bed, I drag the sheet with me until I'm standing in front of him and try to capture his eyes with my own. "I don't know for a hundred percent, but the way you smile in your sleep, it's just the way Rosie does. And her eyes, sometimes it's like I'm staring right into your—"

"But she's not mine," he reminds me of what I told him as he comes to stand next to me.

"That's the thing." My cry breaks out because I can't

escape the reality anymore. "The thing is now..." My voice is unsteady, and a new set of tears sting my eyes.

Grayson shakes his head as if he knows another bombshell is coming.

"Yesterday, Adam showed up at my house, and he told me something that makes it... quite possible that..."

His eyes widen, waiting for my words.

"He doesn't think he's capable of biologically having a child, which means that Rosie isn't his."

The audible exhale from Grayson brings a short silence in this situation.

"She's mine." His whisper comes out as he collapses on the edge of the bed, and I step to him to touch his shoulder as the news sinks in.

"It's very possible that she's yours, and if she isn't then he... fuck. He now wants to be involved with her." More tears fall, and Grayson glances at me, still in a state of shock, yet he touches my arm to comfort me from that revelation.

Our eyes meet, and I don't know who's hurting more right now.

"I don't understand. So you just found out?"

I bite my bottom lip and breathe deep, knowing the hardest part of the conversation is coming. I try to close my eyes to calm my tears, and it works briefly, yet my throat still feels cracked.

"I know they said how far I was along, and it didn't add up to when you and I were together, but they can never be a hundred percent accurate."

"You said the ultrasound showed that you were too far along to even think Rosie could have been mine." His tone has an edge to it.

"I know, and it's true if what they confirmed is correct.

But Rosie… they had to induce me because she didn't want to come out and was late. What if…"

I know what I've done, and the tears fall again because I should have pushed harder for the truth.

"What if what?" Grayson's anger is beginning to boil as he hops off the bed.

"What if she wasn't late at all, just early because… she's yours."

His hands come to his face and he scrubs them across his skin as he takes in my words.

I can only continue while I have a chance since he's quiet. "I never had proof, only a doubt inside of me that I've never been able to shake."

"A doubt you should have fucking told me!" His voice raises, and I know he has every right to be furious, but it scares me how upset he may be, and I still need to lay it all on the table.

He grabs more clothes to throw on, every piece grabbed by a sharp movement.

"You were so relieved when I told you that she wasn't yours, so busy and going places with work. It seemed like fate was giving us our answer. Maybe that's why when she was born, I buried the doubt. I didn't want to ruin your life."

He laughs bitterly. "You kept me away from my daughter for three years. Three fucking years! Why—no, *what* would make you think that I would never want to know that?"

"I don't know for sure. She may not be yours, and then I will have upset you for no reason, but I can't hold it in anymore if we have any chance of a future."

He yanks his shirt on, and I quickly throw the sheet off to slip on some clothes.

"Well, we are definitely going to find out." He's fuming,

and I don't even know how to calm him. "Why wouldn't you want to know? For three years, you've kept this secret. Fuck."

"I'm scared of the answer, okay!" I shout out.

We both look at one another, and I know this is only the start of many turbulent days ahead.

I explain further since I have nothing to lose. "If she's yours then I would have ruined your dreams, your life away from here. You would have felt obliged to return. I don't want to be an obligation. That's why I always kept the uncertainty to myself. If we find out she's yours now, then I've still ruined your life because you've missed three years of her life. And if she isn't yours, then I hate that my mind always casts this doubt inside of me because I can't let you go. It's like I needed some hope that you and I would always be tied together."

He stares at me blankly, and the heavy silence makes me feel like I may drown.

He blows out a breath. "I've made mistakes, you've made mistakes, but one thing I can tell you is that we don't need a kid to be tied together. But this little secret just fucking loosened the rope."

I can only answer with tears falling as I nod slowly.

The overbearing silence returns. We are both now dressed, and a thick air sits between us, each waiting for the other to speak to break the awkwardness.

"I need space. I need to process this, and I need the damn answer. Give me some time and we'll figure out how to get that."

"Of course," I instantly answer.

He curses under his breath as he opens the door, and I follow him.

By the time we reach the bottom of the stairs an oblivious Helen is waiting with a tray. She clearly had high hopes for

us, as the tray has a rose, a plate of pastries, and two cham-
pagne glasses filled with orange juice.

"Heard you both stayed last night and thought you two
love birds may want a little romantic breakfast in bed." Her
cheery tone and smile fades when she seems to grasp that we
are not the same couple who went into that room last night.

"Not a great time, Helen," Grayson snaps.

"Oh, well, no need for that tone, Grayson Blisswood," she
chides.

I mouth *sorry* to her as Grayson continues his warpath
outside, and I follow behind.

The cloudy morning matches the somber mood that I
created.

"Fucking unbelievable." He looks to the sky.

"I'm so sorry."

"Are you?" He doubts me, and I get it.

"Yes," I remain firm.

"The thing is, if Rosie is mine, then you let her down
too."

The sting is too much and now I'm fuming. "You think
this is easy for me? Fuck, I am laying everything on the line
for some ridiculous thought in my head. I know what I've
done to you and her. But she ended up with a good life
regardless, you got the career of your dreams, and I'm trying
to make this right."

He pinches the bridge of his nose. "I can't go in a circle
right now. We'll talk later."

"Yeah, when we both calm down, we will." I step to him,
slightly enraged, and jab his chest which surprises him.
"Either way, Grayson, someone is going to take Rosie away
from me, and you want to know the fucked-up part? We
would have known all this if *your* father didn't hide the
fucking letter."

Grayson's jaw tightens as he freezes. "What did you just say?"

I look away and then back to Grayson, realizing I made a low blow, but he needs all of the truth. "Adam's lawyer delivered a letter a few months ago, and apparently your father signed for it, posing as my own father. Needless to say, neither one of us saw the letter. And I don't even care about that. Do you want to know why?" I push him gently to grab his focus on my words.

"Ask me why," I say, raising my voice.

He seems at a loss of how to process all these facts. "You tell me, B, because it can't get more turbulent than it already is this morning." He cynically smiles to himself.

"I don't care about the letter because at least I now know that Rosie and I aren't the reason that made you return."

He hisses a small chortle. "Looks like you got your wish." He storms to his car, and I watch as he drives off.

———

"I FUCKED UP," I admit my defeat as I sink into the sofa while Kelsey looks on, still in disbelief. Rosie went to bed for the night, and I've been a mess the whole day.

"I don't understand. Is it even possible with all the modern medicine to get it wrong?" She perches against a propped arm.

"If you sleep with two guys in a certain timeframe and use birth control with both, then yes, there is a chance." I feel almost ashamed, but there were four weeks that passed between Adam and Grayson. "I never discussed paternity tests, because when they said how far along I was, then it was a clear answer. When Rosie was born, all that mattered was that she was healthy. I didn't care that she was late and tiny."

"Or she wasn't really late but early?"

"Exactly." I bring a throw pillow to my chest and lament. "He will never forgive me."

She touches my arm to comfort me. "You don't know that. Let him cool down and first get an answer."

"The only thing I can do is wait for him. I'm not going to push him."

"A good plan."

"Do you think I'm horrible person? I mean, I even broke the news in the room that we probably conceived our daughter... if she is his."

She shakes her head and squeezes my arm. "A perfect circle then, and no, I don't. Probably should have told him sooner, but maybe if Rosie is his then you two have every reason to try and be a family. If she isn't, then maybe he will see why you didn't want to make a big deal out of your doubts. I don't know, I want to believe it's all salvageable. You two are that once-in-a-lifetime kind of couple. We all want to root for you."

"I doubt his brothers will be rooting for me now."

Kelsey shrugs her shoulders. "One step at a time."

I nod and know I have a few hard days ahead.

Because there has to be a reason for everything.

20

GRAYSON

Bennett slides a mug of coffee my way where I'm sitting at my kitchen counter with my brothers. Dropping Lucy off at school was an odd silence; she picked up that I wasn't my usual self and she leveled down the snark to zero, and when that happens, then I know I must be sending off desperation vibes.

Explaining everything to Bennett and Knox, they look between one another and neither one of them wants to bite the bullet for offering advice.

"Want something stronger?" Bennett checks as he drinks from his own coffee across from me at the kitchen island.

Looking up from my mug, I shake my head no. It's still morning and I need a clear head.

"*So* you are most likely a dad... That's kind of... cool?" Knox awkwardly states or asks as he looks on, perched on the kitchen counter.

Me, a father? I still can't figure out if it scares me, because I'm beginning to think that it's the least of my issues in this whole situation.

All night, I laid awake thinking of everything that Brooke

told me. I thought about everything that I've missed, imagined a future with Rosie in it and Brooke as the mother of my child.

I've been in this situation before, for a span of a sentence when Brooke called me four years ago. There was only joy bouncing inside of me. Now it's an excitement that I could call Rosie my own.

"Have you spoken to her yet?" Bennett asks as he scratches his stubbled face.

"No, not yet. I needed to simmer down," I admit as I sink back on the barstool.

"Have you simmered down?" Knox asks.

Sighing, I think I have cooled off slightly. The wound is still there, that she didn't tell me sooner, but it isn't as bad as yesterday when a whole damn bottle of salt was poured on it.

"I have a right to be mad, don't I?"

"Sure, but that's not going to help you get an answer. And it's Brooke. Do you really think she kept it from you to hurt you?" Bennett gives me a sympathetic look.

"Three years I've missed," I state again for what feels like the hundredth time.

Noticing Knox giving me a reluctant look, I know he has an opinion about this whole situation, and it causes me to focus my eyes into his direction.

"First get an answer before you head down that road. Also…"

"Say it," I urge.

"Remember that if Rosie isn't yours, Brooke will still be a mess. She has to deal with the other dude who decided he suddenly wants to be involved. That can't be a walk in the park."

Huffing a breath, I know he's right. "I know but… I'm not sure I can get over this."

A snicker escapes Bennett, and I move my sight to his direction.

"You're going to have to. I don't think either one of you are moving houses anytime soon, plus I know you. Can you walk away from her so easily? No, you can't. You've been chasing her in your dreams for years, and now you finally have the chance. So, if you want to throw it all away then be my guest. But you can't, and that is one bet that I'll wager on."

"He's right," Knox adds. "Find a way to co-exist no matter the answer. Don't make it worse for Rosie and yourself." He plays with this string bracelet he has tied on his wrist that he got when he traveled a while back.

"We're here for you." Bennett pats my shoulder, and I give him an appreciative look.

It dawns on me the other fact that we've all just glassed over. "Why do you think Dad did it?"

Bennett and Knox look at one another and neither of them have an answer, but of course Knox isn't afraid to attempt to try to solve the mystery.

"He will have had his reasons. I guess we know why he made you Lucy's guardian."

My head perks up at his sentence because it feels like a puzzle piece clicking. It wasn't until the week before he passed that I was informed he had made me Lucy's guardian. He knew I wouldn't say no and that I would return to Bluetop for her.

"That's typical Grayson and Dad," Bennett says, smirking to himself for the first time since I shared the news. "Silently finding ways to push each other into all things good."

"Give it time, Grays," Knox says, "it'll all come together the way it should. Just don't dig a deeper hole, find a way to climb out of it." He offers his sage advice, and I wonder when he became such an optimist.

"I need an answer." I feel like I've said this on repeat to my brothers and in my mind.

"Then go get it and stop wallowing. There is someone next door who I promise wants clarity as much as you." Knox is firm, and I feel like he's trying a tough-love approach.

I slap my hand on the counter. "I'll go now."

———

BROOKE ANSWERS the door with wet hair and clothes thrown on. She must have been in the shower. I figured she would have called in sick, because if I'm a mess then I doubt she feels different.

"Hey," she greets me with equal parts hope and worry.

The worst part about this moment is that although I ache right now from what feels like a betrayal, she is still so fucking beautiful, and there's this hope that taunts me inside that I don't know how to handle.

"Hey, I won't be long. Just wanted to let you know that I think we should do the paternity test as soon as possible, then we can get the answers by the end of the week." I run my finger along my chin.

"Of course, I already looked into it… I want the answer too." She can't look at me, and maybe it's because I haven't touched her or she's sensing my hesitation.

"I know this isn't easy," I try and find a middle point with her.

My eyes wander to the floor because we're standing here and it feels like we're two strangers. I'm not sure what to say, as there's so much.

"I want to know everything that I've missed." I step

closer to her then begin to ramble. "And maybe we should discuss child support and how the whole living together or custody part would work. I'll start a college fund, and we can change her name on the birth certificate—"

Brooke's palm comes up to stop me, and a subtle amused look graces her face. "Whoa, you have a lot of thoughts happening there. You thought about all of that already?"

I smile to myself. "In the thirty seconds it took to cross the driveway from my place to yours, yeah, I did."

"Grays, is being a dad even what you want?" Her question grabs my full attention, and I'm taken aback and slightly disappointed too.

"You and I were heading somewhere, and I knew you were a package deal. Was I complaining?"

She tilts her head to the side and presses her lips together before letting a breath escape. "No. But being her real father is…" She trails off because she can't put her thought into words.

I can only imagine she wants to say it changes the playing field slightly. Inside, I want to scream no, it doesn't, because I knew a future with Brooke meant one with Rosie, and I never considered the non-biological fact because her father isn't in the picture… and now that can change.

This wait is agony already and we still have days to go.

"What I mean is, will you ever be able to forgive me?" She frowns, and I can see a layer of moisture haze over her eyes.

Glancing away, I breathe in some strength. "I could never hate you, B. I kind of get where you're coming from, and that's a big ask of me. But in the end, you're waiting for an answer too."

A tear slides down her face, and she hiccups a sound. "What if this is the end for us?"

I can't take this; I step to her and pull her into my arms for a hug to soothe her and to fulfill a selfish need to touch her and inhale her scent. I rub my hand in circles on her back while she clings to my shirt and her cries are muffled into my chest.

"You and I don't do closure," I remind her.

After a minute, she pulls back and wipes away her tears. Seeing her like this is awful, and even when I went away to college, making it clear my life wouldn't be returning to Bluetop and I knew she was trying to hide her tears that I caused, it wasn't as painful as this.

"We'll wait, okay?" I pinch the bridge of my nose and know I need to get out of here before I do something that won't help the situation. Angry sex is definitely flashing across my brain, because that's the best way I like to calm her and the way I like to work out some stress.

Turning to walk away, I glance over my shoulder. "Yeah, to better answer your question, I want to do the whole father thing. That's the easiest part about all of this."

"And you know that my doubt was more a wish than anything."

"Hopefully two people wishing the same thing makes it come true then." I nod to her before I walk away, and it feels like I'm walking into a gray cloud, because I don't have the answer about what will happen to Brooke and me.

21

GRAYSON

"**A**nother lap, let's go," I tell the boys of the baseball team as they run, breathing ragged. Admittedly, I am taking out my frustration and stress from waiting for the results on them.

It's been a few days since we sent everything off to get the answers, and I've been doing everything to keep myself busy and distracted. Hell, I even volunteered to help Knox with the animals, and I was never one with chickens or horses.

I clap my hands together. "Faster, come on, pick up the slack," I shout.

Last time I was dragged here, now I volunteered. Anything to keep me out of the house and away from accidentally seeing Brooke, or even worse, Rosie, because I know I wouldn't be able to keep my eyes away.

Coach looks at me with an almost stern look. "Everything okay there, Grays? You're pushing them a little hard."

"Am I? Thought you wanted a winning team," I reply, with my eyes set on the field as I cross my arms.

He chuckles at me. "True that, but you seem in a mood. Anything I can help you with?"

I give him side-eye. The guy has no idea. Nobody can help me right now.

"Okay, give me the silent treatment, just don't keep it inside or you're going to kill one of these guys in the process, and I need them to be able to keep down Rosemary's home-made granola bars that she delivered." His thumb shoots in the direction of the team that is finishing their lap with heavy breathing.

I hold my hands up in understanding.

"You coming to team dinner this week? Rosemary is making lasagna," he asks as he occupies himself with making a roster for the next game.

"Probably not this week. You really still do dinner every week?"

Coach shrugs it off like it's no big deal. "Sure, some of these boys aren't lucky enough to get homecooked meals, as their parents work too much, or some just need to experience a family dinner every now and then. Plus, Rosemary and I have one son who is grown and gone, but we weren't done raising more. Every now and then there's someone who we informally foster in a way. You don't need the same blood or even paperwork to be family."

A scoff escapes me, because leave it to Coach to give the words of wisdom to fit the scene that he has no idea is unravelling in my life—it's his gift.

"You always know what to say, Coach." I refocus my attention on the boys who are all drinking from their water bottles. I cup my hands around my mouth and raise my voice, "Okay, throwing practice, take your positions."

His food for thought will just have to wait.

———

RETURNING TO THE HOUSE, my eyes catch Lucy hopping out of Drew's truck, and maybe it's everything else this week has thrown at me or maybe it is literally no brother wants to see his sixteen-year-old sister with a nineteen-year-old guy, but the rage in me boils just enough.

I press my foot on the pedal a little harder than necessary to make my arrival into the driveway known, but I'm too late and he's driving away. Lucy is casually walking to the front door with her backpack on.

Sliding out of my car and slamming the door, my control button is fully off. "What the hell was that?" I call out to my sister.

She turns to me with a glare on her face. "A ride, relax."

"Fuck that. You don't ride in cars with guys, let alone guys who are not even in high school. Besides, what happened to studying at Kendall's house?" I raise my eyebrows at her because she is completely busted.

"Seriously, chill out. I had a change of plans and Drew offered me a ride."

I feel my nostrils flare and I tap my foot, as I don't like this scenario in the slightest. "Prince Charming, I'm sure. This doesn't happen again, do you understand?"

She plants her hands on her hips and her look is unimpressed. "This is so unfair. If Dad had gone with the original plan, then I would have at least been stuck with Bennett or Knox. I bet they wouldn't go Cujo on me right now."

I groan to myself as I run a hand through my hair. "Well, guess what, Dad fucked us all over, so here I am." I splay my hands out like I'm a prize.

"What the fuck does that mean?" Lucy looks at me almost disgusted with my statement.

I can't drag her into my mess, even though she's smart and knows something is up. "Forget it, okay. Just get inside and I'll order some food or something."

She drops her bag with purpose to the ground at her feet. "What? I thought for sure we would get a Brooke dinner tonight. We haven't seen her all week."

A long exhale escapes me. "It's just us tonight, okay?"

Lucy crosses her arms and lifts her head at me in inspection. "What did you do?"

I laugh to myself. "This one isn't me. Trust me."

"Are you avoiding her? Because that's really low."

"Not avoiding her, we're just..." Before I'm able to finish the sentence, a chirpy voice sings my name.

"Grayson!"

Lucy and I turn our heads to see Rosie running out of the front door of their house, with Brooke trailing behind her throwing a sweater on. "Rosie, I said wait."

Brooke looks up from Rosie's path to see me and Lucy standing on the receiving end.

"Grays! I made something for you." Rosie wiggles a piece of paper in her hand as she runs to me.

I bend down so I'm at eye level with her and get ready to block her finish line, as she sometimes forgets how to stop her speed. My arms are open to catch her, and the moment she enters my bubble, I bask in the warmth of her little hug.

This little girl has a spot in my life. I'm not sure what title I'll have—neighbor, friend... dad—but there's room for her in my heart, and I breathe her in like she's mine.

Brooke comes running after and stops a good distance from me. "Rosie, I said to wait, and you can put it in Grayson's mailbox before we go for a walk."

"But Grays is here, so I don't need to mail him my

picture." Rosie smiles as she hands me her little work of art made from crayons.

How can I not soften and offer Rosie a warm smile? "This is pretty." My eyes study the drawing, and although the scribble is very rough, I vaguely sense they're people. Maybe she had one of her teachers help with the outlines.

"It's you, Mommy, Lucy, and me," she tells me proudly.

"Where's Jelly?" I inquire, surprised the stuffed animal didn't make the A-team for her drawing.

She slants her shoulders up to her ears. "I didn't have time to add her."

"Well, I'm honored to have been included in your drawing."

"When people don't feel good, we make them drawings. Mommy said you weren't feeling well, that's why you have stayed at your house," she innocently explains, and my eyes shoot to Brooke who gives me an awkward shrug.

My eyes scan to Lucy who has wide eyes, curious to the scene playing out in front of her.

Standing up, I ruffle her hair and answer softly, "You know, kiddo, I'm feeling pretty okay now." Seeing Rosie is that feel-good hug that everyone needs in their life. "I get to keep this?"

She nods her head in excitement.

"It'll look perfect on our fridge."

"Hey, Rosie, can I see?" Lucy asks, and I know it's to give Brooke and me a moment more than anything else.

Rosie runs over to Lucy, which leaves me and Brooke to stare at one another in our unknown state.

"Sorry, I told her… well, I didn't know what to say, so I thought the old sick excuse was the way to go." Brooke tucks her hands into her jeans pockets as she bites the corner of her lip.

"It's okay. We can talk to her after we know… well, when we have our answer."

"Right, any day now. I guess Lucy doesn't know?"

I shake my head and scratch the back of my neck. "No, she's smart enough to know something is up."

"I figured you hadn't told her when she texted me earlier asking if I could help her with an outfit choice for…" Brooke stops when she realizes she's about to let something slip. A knowing grin spreads across her face.

"Tell me it's not for a guy whose name is Drew?"

Brooke brings her fingers to her lips and pretends to zip them. Then she gently tags my arm. "Relax, I think it's for her driving test."

"That may be worse." I can't help but let a smirk form on my face.

The last thirty seconds has almost put me at ease because that's just Brooke's ability to calm me.

"Anyhow, Rosie and I will leave you guys alone. We're going for a walk to burn off some energy. I would invite you to come with, but I think we both need some space."

"Probably best."

Our eyes don't move as we stand locked in a gaze.

"I'll let you know when it's delivered tomorrow."

I gulp at the timeline. "Tomorrow," I barely say.

Who knew an envelope could change so much, but it already feels like my life is about to be upended.

22

BROOKE

I'm pacing my living room at high speed. Another day this week that I called in sick, but there is nothing I could possibly do that would keep me focused at work. My phone pinged bright and early in the morning letting me know that I should expect a delivery today and I need to sign for it, so here I am on my third cup of cold tea because I keep forgetting to drink from the damn mug.

Honestly, I could throw up from nerves, and nothing feels remotely normal right now. Today our lives will change, Rosie's especially, although she has no clue. I've been running through scenarios all week and have barely slept in days.

Giving space to Grayson hurt like a knife to my chest, but I know it was the right thing to do. We all need to process.

It wasn't a great feeling when I was at the grocery store and heard one of the kids from the high school complaining about Grayson's hard-love approach at practice. Or hearing Sally-Anne mention that Grayson snapped when she ran out of bagels the other day.

I know I'm responsible, that I've turned Bluetop's golden boy into a momentary villain.

My phone vibrates and immediately my eyes dart to the screen, but disappointment hits me when I see that it's only Kelsey with a text message.

KELSEY

Hang in there. I'm here if you need anything. I'll close the salon early.

It's okay. Kind of have to speak to one of them and that may take a while.

I don't even know how to label it anymore. Exes, possible dads, future co-parent. I groan out some stress.

It feels like hours until my doorbell rings, but I think it was only twenty minutes more. Signing for the envelope with haste, I wait for the delivery man to return to his truck before I stare at the yellow envelope and freeze.

I'm not sure the best way to do this. Does it need to be some ceremonial procedure, or do I just rip it open? Maybe I should do it with Grayson?

Heat hits my face and I feel like my body is about to give out to the point I may faint.

But I push on, and I begin to break open the seal—until my phone disrupts my focus. I see the name of Rosie's preschool flash across the screen, and they never phone.

I answer quickly, and the lady on the other end speaks. "Ms. Rivers? I think you need to come down to the school. We have a little issue with Rosie."

I do not hesitate or want to waste a moment. "I'll be right there." I hang up, realizing I forgot to ask what the issue is. Adrenaline spikes into high gear and I feel almost lightheaded. Because moms have superpowers, I move into action mode.

I tuck the envelope in my purse and grab my car keys.

Rushing out to my garage, Grayson's voice mixes with the door opening.

"Brooke, was that the delivery man?"

"Not now, Grayson. Rosie's school phoned and something happened. I need to get to her." My voice is shaky because I've never had this happen.

He must grasp my position or maybe it's concern that overpowers him too. "Give me your keys, I'll drive." His tone is insistent, and even though today of all days is not the day to drag him further into my life until that damn paper gets read, I know he won't let me say no, and truthfully, I may need him right now.

———

WE SIT on the small chairs made for children as we wait for Ms. Justina. There was no time for Grayson and me to talk, as he pretty much broke every traffic violation of Bluetop and the state to get us here.

Truthfully, we look ridiculous as two adults sitting in pint-sized chairs, waiting in anticipation for what feels like a visit to the principal's office. They assured me Rosie wasn't hurt and was feeling well and that's not why they asked me to come in.

Ms. Justina arrives to the room with a cheery look as she straightens her tunic over her leggings, her red hair in a pony-tail. She was a few years ahead of us at school, but she's a Bluetop native.

She gives us a polite smile before she sits down on the only adult-sized chair behind the table and rests her hands on the table. "Oh, I didn't realize you would be coming with someone, let alone Grayson Blisswood, but Helen did mention the other day at the farmers market that sparks may be flying again between you two." She focuses her attention on Grayson, and I swear she's giving him flirty eyes. "Or is it just rumor?"

I really don't have time for a mid-thirty-year-old drooling over Grayson right now. "Shall we focus on my daughter, or would you like to give us the latest on your divorce?" I snipe back, because today is not the day to mess with this mama bear.

Grayson looks at me, almost impressed with my feistiness.

"Why, thank you, Brooklyn, for the reminder, but yes, let's focus on Rosie. You see, she has been acting a little out of sorts lately."

"What do you mean?" I press for more details.

"Well, we've always been *sensitive* to the fact that she doesn't have a father figure in her life. Many kids come from different family shapes; she isn't the first."

I cringe at the direction of where this conversation is going. "Your point being?"

"Lately, Rosie mentioned a monster a few times, then the fact that she would be getting a daddy since her mother has a boyfriend. I could understand that the dynamics might be confusing for her, but that's just life and kids are resilient. But we can't tolerate her pushing other kids, and that's what happened when Jabez mentioned to Rosie that she doesn't have a father—"

"First off," Grayson says, holding a finger up, "who the hell names their kid Jabez?"

"That couple who moved here from Portland and opened a coffee shop," Justina shrugs.

Grayson continues to question. "Good for them. Did their little monster provoke Rosie?"

"I mean, yes, but we don't answer with fists, we answer with words."

Grayson doesn't give me any chance to respond as he continues his exchange with Justina. "Agreed, now let's ask ourselves where Rosie would have learned to push someone?" He raises his brows at Justina in a challenge.

Her face turns slightly snooty. "Normally children react based on what they see at home—"

My palm flies up to stop her. "Never once has Rosie pushed or seen anyone push someone on purpose at home, so don't you dare suggest it's my parenting."

"I'm not, well, I mean, it must be hard to do to raise her all on your own. How can you be sure she never does it at home?"

My voice cracks in astonishment. "What? She pushes her stuffed animals? She has no siblings. Who in the world would she be pushing? I can assure you she didn't learn it from me."

Except the one time that I playfully pushed my frisky boyfriend away in the kitchen with a beaming smile on my face.

Justina tries to calm me with hand gestures which only fumes me more. "I'm not suggesting that, only that perhaps something in your parenting can be tweaked."

Grayson lets a sarcastic laugh escape. "That is enough. Brooke does an amazing job with Rosie, and if this has never come up before, then maybe you should check who she's hanging out with on the playground. Maybe you should talk to the parents of Jilez, Jesel—"

"Jabez," she corrects him.

"Exactly. Now, I think you need to tone it down with the finger-pointing and apologize to Brooke, because I can guarantee that Rosie couldn't be receiving a kinder upbringing."

My lips tug into a smile from his words—not even his words, it's his tone of confidence and persistence that has me in knots.

"I do apologize. I was just raising a concern because it's never happened before. Maybe it's all the changes at home if you two are…"

"Listen," I say, reaffirming my opinion, "it doesn't matter what goes on in my romantic life. What matters is Rosie has me."

"Okay, and what about her telling the kids that she is getting a father. I don't want to encourage it if it's something in her make-believe world."

"It's not pretend," Grayson interjects. "She has a father, and I would appreciate it if you change your tone when you speak to the mother of my child and to me." He says it so adamantly.

My mouth gapes open in astonishment of what he just said, because we don't know. Instead, he just declared he is Rosie's father to Justina, who looks shocked but ready to spread the gossip like wildfire.

"Oh? I didn't realize." She gulps.

A gulp is a lot more than I am able to muster in this moment, because I am completely speechless and at a loss for what to do or how to react.

"I think this conversation is over. Shall we take Rosie home or can she finish the day?" Grayson abruptly stands and waits for an answer.

It takes a few seconds for Justina to digest this scene, and I'm still not sure I will be able to stand.

"Uhm, no, it's fine. Rosie, she can, uh, stay."

"Great. I'll assume the matter is settled." He looks at me and his head tilts subtly to the direction of the exit.

———

WE'RE SITTING in my car in the parking lot, with me in the passenger's seat, without having said a word. But now I'm breaking that spell.

"What the hell, Grayson? Why would you do that? We don't even know for sure." I'm furious but keep my tone as neutral as possible, because this has volcano-sized repercussions.

"I know." He rests his head against his propped elbow on the window.

"Literally, by dinner time everyone in this town will know what you just said. Not to mention Lucy and Rosie. What would possess you to do that?"

"Because it's what I want." His head snaps to my direction and our eyes lock.

I can't answer, as in a way it all almost feels like a sweet gesture.

"I'm sorry, but I couldn't stand the way she spoke to you and something in me snapped. This protectiveness that I didn't know I had." His face is apologetic, and I can see he is in conflict because he knows what he did.

Today isn't the day to have an argument either, as we have enough on our plates. "Papa bear instinct." I attempt a weak smile. "Parents get a little crazy sometimes."

"No shit. Someone named their child Jabez."

His serious-toned answer makes me laugh and cry at the same time because, wow, what a ridiculous name, but it's preventing us from combusting into a complete waterfall of tears and for that I am thankful.

"Really, B, what is this preschool with Justina and Jabez, and I swear I saw a poster that there is a vegetable of the week and it's freaking cabbage. Who does that to a kid?"

I can only smile more at his terrified look over cabbage. "Bluetop only has one preschool, so it has to work, and she likes it."

He shakes his head, and as much as his subtle grin is calming as we soak in a little silence, we now need to know our truth.

"I got the letter."

His look turns serious. "And?"

"We need to open it. Maybe not here but somewhere private. It's time."

He answers by quickly starting my car and driving us off.

———

HE PULLS to the side of the dirt road outside of town into a spot among a small forest, and I know why he picked this spot. It was once a place we would go to on the regular as teenagers. He would park his truck and we would lose track of time with each other.

We were so hopeful.

And today is no different, except the sun is out and it's late morning, with our lives about to change.

Getting out of the car, we both walk to the back of his SUV and lean against the trunk. My hand shakes as I pull out the envelope from my purse.

"I won't run away if you need me, even if Rosie isn't mine," he informs me, and it causes me to look up in surprise. "I don't have an answer for us, but I won't let her down, I'll adopt her."

Words get stuck in my throat at his proclamation. He isn't

thinking clearly, but I can't get into it because we need to move on with this.

I can only nod at his words and not question it. "And you know that there is only one way I want this to go, and either way, I am so sorry."

He returns by answering with a gentle nod.

We both watch my hands fumble with the seal before I pull out the paper.

The moment I read the paper. I drop my hand, with tears swelling in my eyes, as I enter a new, unsure world.

"She's yours, Grayson."

23

GRAYSON

I feel like a man who's made it to the top of a mountain. The relief floods me and the pride overtakes me. I'm a father now.

Instantly, I pull Brooke into a hug and keep her in my arms for a solid minute as we both take in the confirmation. Her hands run along my back, and I kiss the top of her head.

"She's mine, really mine. We're parents, together. Rosie is mine. Ours, actually." I whisper it out loud, all my shock mixed with happiness.

She tips her head back to study my face but stays rooted in my arms. "Ours."

Christ, this week, I've seen her with so many variations of tears that I was beginning to think I needed to start a manual to keep track of all the emotions, but now she clearly has happy tears as she blows out a calming breath.

Stepping away, we both lean against my car again as we look straight ahead.

"What now?"

"Well, I should probably stop crying for the first time in a week," she attempts to joke as she wipes away a tear with the back of her hand.

I nudge her with my shoulder; I couldn't agree more. "Definitely that."

"Wow, I guess there is a whole list of things, and it starts with informing Adam so he can put that topic to rest and telling… Rosie."

"I guess I kind of speeded up our need to tell her?" My face squinches as I recall my outburst at her preschool.

A wry smile forms on her face. "Considering they already sent me an e-mail in the car asking if I should add you as the emergency contact then yes. Yes, we need to tell her."

"Okay, tonight. I will talk to my brothers and Lucy this afternoon." I angle my body to her and brush some of her hair behind her ear, her eyes beautifully damp. "And you absolutely should add me to the emergency contact list, then tell me who the hell to contact to ensure a real vegetable gets onto that weekly board."

She snorts a laugh, because in this moment, we have every reason to be elated. "I think one of the moms from the parents' committee picked the vegetable of the week—the mother of Jabez."

Now I have to laugh, because leave it to us to slowly emerge from this week with a smile on our faces.

———

LUCY LOOKS at me in awe at the news that I just shared with my brothers and sister in my living room. They're sitting in a row on the sofa while I pace the rug.

"No wonder you were an asshole all week. So, I'm like an aunt?" Lucy smiles at me, with her hands coming to her face to try and hide her shock.

"I guess since I'm a dad, then yeah, that makes you an aunt."

I'm a father to a daughter. Rosie is mine. I can't stop repeating it because this is the news I wanted.

"Does this mean I can't charge for babysitting anymore since Rosie is my niece?" Lucy gives me a teasing look, but I can see she's excited for me.

"I can't believe we have another generation of Blisswoods. I feel like we need to do something to celebrate." Bennett hasn't stopped smiling for me.

"Let me first tell Rosie with Brooke. I'm going over there soon." And I'm nervous. Not much in life wrecks me with nerves, but who knew picking out the right shirt to impress a three-year-old would be what makes me come undone.

"Does this mean I'm getting shipped to live with one of the other brothers?" Lucy asks slightly in doubt but also still in good spirits.

Knox pulls her ponytail. "Hey, we are more than just the *other* brothers."

This is where I know our family meeting may get slightly awkward. "No, no change on the living situation. Well, I don't know. But you won't get shipped off."

Bennett's eyes squint and his smile fades. "Wait, are you and Brooke still on a break?"

I run my tongue along my bottom lip and flop onto the recliner. "We need time. The focus should be telling Rosie right now and letting her adapt to the idea."

"But you two are so good together," Lucy offers her insight.

"And we will be a part of one another's lives for eternity, that's not going to change."

"Don't do this." Knox stands and shakes his head at me, his hands forming fists at his sides as if he needs to control his feelings. "You're an absolute idiot. Don't make her wait, because we all know you want to be with her, and she does too. You're just being stubborn and cautious."

"He's right," Bennett says. "You love her, and she loves you. Don't ride the 'I feel angry' train for too long." He throws his feet up on the coffee table.

I look to the clock on the wall and know I need to head over to Brooke's soon. "I hear what you're all saying, but can I just have a little time to process everything?"

"But you seem to be processing the Rosie news just fine. It's Brooke that has you acting a little loco," Lucy blatantly points out.

Bennett indicates to her. "See, that's why she's going to go to a good college. She's smart."

"Let me figure it out. One day at a time, and today is telling Rosie," I implore my family with my smile returning, because in an hour, I will have someone who can call me Dad.

"Since you're in a good mood, does this mean I can have a party after I get my license?" Lucy flashes her eyes at me to push her luck.

Knox slaps my back. "Just think, in thirteen years you get to deal with all of this again."

My stomach drops as it all becomes real.

———

As I CLOSE the door behind me, Brooke rushes to me, looking back at Rosie who is planted on the sofa watching cartoons.

"Ready?" she whispers.

"More than ever."

We agreed that we would keep it simple and not make a big story out of it. Rosie was super chill when she found me mounting her mother in the kitchen, so this should be a piece of cake, *I think.*

I double-check and see that Rosie is deep into her pony movie, which is slightly discouraging, as once she sees those ponies her brain goes into a complete trance.

"Smart move putting the ponies on." I'm sarcastic, because now it feels like I may be climbing a wall to get to her.

Brooke gives me a stern look before wiggling the remote control in the air. "I've got the power, Grays; never hand this thing over to her." She's kind of hot when she says that, maybe because there is a hint of deviousness, only amplified when she holds the remote up and hits the off button.

"Hey," Rosie whines as she snaps back into the normal world.

Brooke grabs my arm, and we walk in Rosie's direction, because this is our opening.

"Sorry, bug, but Grayson is here, and we have something exciting to tell you," Brooke begins as she leads me around the coffee table in front of Rosie. Brooke sits on the floor while I perch on the edge of the sofa next to Rosie.

The kid looks between us, unsure what's happening, which is why she holds Jelly tighter.

"The thing is, we found out something amazing, and we want to share it with you." Brooke affectionately touches Rosie's leg.

"We're getting a pony?"

Brooke and I laugh gently at her thought.

"No, kiddo, you're getting something better," I say, deciding I need to get involved in this conversation.

"It turns out that Grayson… is your daddy." Brooke gently and softly states the news.

We both survey Rosie's face while she listens, and the kid has a good poker face, as we don't get much.

"I only just found out, and it's the best news I could ever have," I add.

Her little head looks at Brooke then me then back to Brooke. "I thought I was magic."

Brooke lovingly looks at our daughter. "You were. I just didn't know that Grayson was… part of the magical potion." A cartoonish look spreads across Brooke's face when she realizes that what she said could be interpreted in many ways.

I chuckle under my breath. "Exactly the magic potion."

Rosie hums as if she's thinking. "So, Grayson is Daddy?"

"Yep, that's me." I touch her shoulder, and I don't care if she needs days to figure this out, because the vision of her wondering about all of this is too adorable. This little girl will be able to wrap me around her little finger, I know it.

"Then Daddy is moving in?" A smile spreads across her little face.

Brooke and I look at one another awkwardly.

"You know, right now we just want to get to know us as a family, and we can do that with Grayson living next door," Brooke explains, with her eyes double-checking with me as she says every word.

"What does that mean?" Rosie inquires, with her little eyes scanning both of us.

"Lots of picnics, I'll pick you up from school sometimes, dinner together. Anything you want," I offer.

Rosie's entire body perks up and her eyes turn to little saucers as her smile widens. "Like ice cream and tea parties in the playhouse? A swing?"

Brooke and I shake our heads, entertained with Rosie, but you can only ask so much from a three-and-a-half-year-old.

"Sure." I know I'm agreeing to the first of her many requests.

She claps her hands together, excited. "I have a daddy," she coos.

"Yeah, kiddo, that's me."

Looking to Brooke, I know we have conquered the first step, and now I know I need to address what happens to us.

24

BROOKE

M y foot propels me forward and back on my porch swing as I read a book under the light over the front door. It's a beautiful late-spring evening. I shouldn't be in this peaceful of a state, but I'm trying.

The other week, I got answers, had a quick, easy conversation with Adam and wished him luck, but the best part was seeing Rosie's face light up at the news that Grayson is her dad.

Grayson and I have kept conversations and texts about Rosie. He and Lucy came over for dinner last night, and he took Rosie to the park this morning. We'll figure out the parenting stuff together as we go.

Maybe I should be more hesitant to let Grayson in, but I owe him for lost time, and nothing inside me, not even the corners of my soul, give me an inclination that he won't put Rosie first.

Us, on the other hand, I'm not sure.

It's as if he's avoiding the conversation, beyond affectionate touches as two parents. Nothing has given me an indication that we have a chance, but nothing has shown me we don't either.

Patience is all I can give, and I'm doing my best to wait it out.

My eyes peer up at Grayson making strides in my direction, away from his house where there are a few extra cars and the subtle sound of music.

"Rosie asleep?" he asks as he slides next to me on the swing.

"Yeah, all of the excitement from the last week has made her sleep like a bear the past few nights." I set my book to the side table and take in the air and the feeling of Grayson sitting next to me—close.

His head tilts to the direction of his house. "Thought it's best to escape."

"I still can't believe you're letting Lucy have a party."

"It's not a party, it's a gathering," he corrects me. "It was either this or let her run the roads wild with her new license. Besides, she deserves it. She's a good kid, and I saw the invite list; not exactly the crowd that I worry about."

I scoff a laugh at his theory. "You really don't remember high school and the *gatherings* we attended."

He looks at me with inquisition.

"Come on, Grays, are there guys there? Alcohol somewhere in the house?"

His face drops. "Shit, I'm going to have to sweep the house in about twenty minutes."

I rub my arm against his. "Or thirty seconds, if we're going by the average time for a teenage boy." Riling Grayson right now just feels natural.

"I wasn't the average teenage boy," he quickly justifies.

"Yeah, above average, I would say." I try to keep a

straight face but it's a struggle, especially when he gives me the look like he wants to prove me wrong.

"Remember Sean O'Grady's party?" His arm moves to rest behind me on the back of the swing.

"How could I forget? It's where you kissed me for the first time," I reminisce. It was the after-party the night Bluetop won an important basketball game. I felt a pair of eyes following me around the moment I arrived, until Grayson found me in the kitchen with a red plastic cup in hand. All week I had been waiting for him to make a move, and he did; he asked if we could go for a walk. "Guess that was the first sign that walks with you always lead to something."

"It's not like it's my signature move," he quips. "But I'm happy it got us alone, in the hammock."

"It did."

We look at one another, and I know that we are both lost in a memory.

"My favorite walk with you is the one that led to Rosie," I admit, because it was his insistence that I have the grand tour that led us to that night.

A grin tugs on his mouth. "Mine too."

He tips his head to mine until our foreheads touch, and his hand slides to the back of my neck. It's the first time that I can breathe him in without tears since this whole ordeal began.

"Don't hate me," I softly request.

"I could never," he promises and retreats back before inviting me to snuggle into his arms as we continue to swing. "I missed seeing you pregnant with our child, all of Rosie's firsts, I don't even know what kind of baby she was," he lists.

"I can't get you those three years back, but I can promise you that the years she will remember only start now, and she was the most beautiful and easiest baby, the perfect gift," I speak as my head leans against his shoulder.

"I would have wanted it differently. A ring on your finger, a house that I would design—hell, I would've been there every step of the way."

"I know you would have, but beyond my apology, I can't go back and change time," I remind him, because I won't keep saying sorry for years to come. "It's up to you to forgive me, but we're in each other's lives, and there is only one way I want it to be."

A sigh escapes him, and I feel his body rise with his breath. "Give me time."

Disgruntled from the circle of this conversation, I stand and walk to the edge of the porch where I cross my arms. "If I hear those words again I may lose my cool. I'm giving you space, what more do you need me to do?"

I hear him stalk after me before he grabs my arm to turn my attention and body to him. His hands grab my face, and he crashes his mouth onto mine, fusing us together, and everything inside me melts.

I've been craving this for days. I forgot how much his mouth has the ability to completely mark me as his.

His hand tangles in my hair as he pulls my head to an angle where he demands more from my lips, his tongue sliding along my own. My moan gets lost between our mouths.

He needs this as much as me, and he kisses me harder.

This better not be a test to see if I still spark something in him; it should be the reminder.

I give it my all and wrap my arms around his neck as I press my body against his. Inside I am screaming to love me, but instead, the message gets transmitted through a kiss that is tipping the axis of the world.

The sounds he makes, *God*, it's a promising start.

Separating our mouths, the tips of our noses nestle.

"I couldn't help myself."

"I'm yours, you don't need to justify it," I remind him. "Well, maybe to the group of teenagers spying on us through the window, but not me." I try to throw in a little humor to this.

He smiles against my mouth before he steals another kiss.

"I shouldn't confuse things," he mentions, and it makes me fear he regrets it. "I'm sorry. No, I'm not. Should I be?"

My hands land on his wrists that craddle my face. "Don't ask me, I'm biased."

"This is my cue to go. Otherwise, I'll do things to you that will complicate the hell out of us. Time is the answer, and if I stay, then I will strip you naked until I'm coming inside of you."

Heat flushes across my face. "It's not complicated, Grays, so don't make us an obstacle." Breaking our contact, I step to the side.

"I'm trying. Listen, I'll go, but don't think this isn't hard for me. I'm at a total loss of how to navigate us again."

"Well, I hope you find the way." I look away, because if my eyes meet his then I will want to plead, beg, and shake him until he shows me that I mean everything to him.

Instead, disappointment comes over me, because I know tonight, I won't get an answer of where we stand.

25

GRAYSON

I throw the pencil across my desk in my home office, unhappy with my design. I've tied up all my final projects from my life in the city, and they offered me the project in Madison, but that doesn't start until the fall. Instead, I'm working on my personal project that nobody knows about.

The dream place with five bedrooms, a big kitchen, and plenty of space outside. It's always been in my head, but now it flows out more than ever. But I'm done for tonight, and there isn't even a trickle of creativity left.

Grabbing my empty glass of soda, I walk down the hall and see that Lucy is in her room. Knocking on her door, I wait for her signal before checking in on her.

"All good?" I ask when she looks up from her desk and laptop.

"Yeah, only one more week of hell, then it's summer. Which is quite possibly only a slight upgrade from hell."

Smirking to myself, I can only imagine what attitude she has going into her first summer with a job. "Working at Olive

Owl is tradition, and babysitting Rosie occasionally isn't so bad, is it?"

She plays with her hair and ties it up into a knot on her head. "Rosie is the fun part; it's reporting to all three of you guys that has me scared."

"We'll go gentle," I promise as I lean against the inner panel of the door.

Lucy looks outside then back to me. "Another storm tonight. You think Rosie is freaking out?"

My body tenses, as I honestly hadn't looked at the forecast, and Lucy makes a solid point. I hate the idea of Rosie being scared, and I know that puts Brooke on edge too.

Walking to the window, I peek through the blinds to check the night sky and see lightning in the distance.

"You can go, I'll be fine," she says. "I have like an hour more of studying then I'll be off to bed."

I look at her and doubt her for a second. "No guys sneaking in?"

She laughs. "Nah, that was the other day when you took Rosie to Olive Owl." She clicks her inner cheek and I know she's messing with me.

In all honesty, I know she's fine. She's been keeping her head in the books since she has finals.

"If you're sure then I'll just go check on them."

She nods. "Super sure."

I touch her back in appreciation as I walk out of the room. "Thanks."

Two minutes later, I'm walking across the lot to Brooke's and already know that I'm in too deep. Since I kissed her the other day, we haven't mentioned it and per usual just focused on Rosie.

The sound of thunder is in the distance, and it only creates a need for me to check on my girls. We haven't discussed boundaries, but I let myself in the way I did before getting the news about Rosie.

Immediately, I notice all the lights are off except for a line of light appearing from under Brooke's bedroom door. Rosie must be sleeping in Brooke's room like she normally does when she's scared.

I push the door ajar, and Brooke looks up. My eyes quickly take in the scene of her sitting up in bed reading on her tablet, and she's in a fucking cotton tank that is my demise every single fucking time. I gulp when I realize that Rosie isn't here.

Brooke and I alone is trouble, and I know it.

"What are you doing here, Grays?" Brooke looks at me, surprised.

I step into her room and close the door, not wanting to wake Rosie. "Sorry, I didn't mean to scare you. I thought Rosie would be frightened with the storms coming and wanted to check on you both." I rub my chin as I try to tear my eyes away from the vision in front of me. "It kind of scares me that you didn't realize I was in the house."

She gives me a simple smile. "I got used to you. You're like the wallpaper in this place. Nothing unusual."

"Right, and Rosie?"

"Hasn't woken yet. But I think the storms are staying off to the north of here." She brings the blanket slightly higher to cover herself, but in the process, it moves up her leg to reveal skin…

This is not what I need right now.

I breathe and feel my mouth water from want.

"Maybe I should check on her." Words come out of my mouth, but my sight is fixed on something I selfishly want right now.

"You can, but she's sound asleep so let's not wake her."

We can't wake her.

Is it wrong if I accept the challenge?

Stepping closer, I know I should be heading in the opposite direction and get out of here. My thoughts are still not clear enough.

"Maybe I should stay a little longer to make sure?"

"Okay, if that's what you want. Let me grab my robe and we can go put on a movie or something," she says as she comes to her knees, the blanket falling to a pool on the mattress, and she reveals that she is literally in a tank and panties.

I snap and charge at her.

Kissing her so hard until she falls back onto the bed.

We haven't had our angry/celebration sex yet, and I think we need it to help me think clearly.

Parting for barely a second to get my shirt off, our hands roam wild, and our mouths take everything we are feeling.

Her legs wrapping around me causes her body to press against my cock that is ready to dive into her pussy and feel her heat.

My fingers sneak under her panties, and she is perfectly ready. Her arousal covers my fingers and I slide them to her clit to draw a pattern that drives her crazy, before dipping inside of her.

I bury her moans by kissing her. If she needs to breathe, she can breathe through me, because I can't stop. We're already tumbling toward our ecstasy. Her hands search for my zipper, and she works quickly to get my pants off.

We aren't going to go slow. We both have a primal need right now, but that doesn't stop me from lowering her tank and taking a nipple into my mouth to suck as her back arches up to me.

She cries in pleasure before she quickly turns her head into the pillow.

"Take me, Grays, do it now," she rasps.

We roll to our sides, a mess of tangled limbs. Then I slide into her with such ease. The first pump causes her to gasp, and the second, she sinks her nails into my skin.

"You feel too good. So fucking wet for me, so needy for me, and it's all mine."

Every stroke feels like a message. We fuck each other with a purpose.

I give her a little swat on the ass, which she answers by kissing my mouth. I know she likes it just as much as I enjoy her pussy tightening around my cock.

Every time I go deep with force, it's both punishment and love, to which she replies by biting into my neck and hanging on like our lives depend on it.

"Take it. It's all yours," she murmurs against my skin as our breathing grows heavy.

It feels like I may spiral out of control, but her eyes locking with my own keeps me centered.

"I'm going to bury myself so deep into you that you will feel me for days."

It causes her to purr and that sends me soaring. My hand travels between us to help her along. This session doesn't take long because it feels like forever since I've sunk myself inside her as she writhes under me.

It's only when we lay there a mess of two sweaty bodies that I realize how much of a selfish bastard I am.

Then I take more as I lie there inside her and she strokes my hair for a few minutes more, with the sound of thunder still in the distance.

"I should go," I mention as I slowly retreat out of her and look for my clothes.

"Oh." The disappointment is apparent.

Understandable, as I've confused her more. "I don't want to give you mixed messages, but this isn't what we should be doing right now." No matter how right it feels.

Glancing over my shoulder as I throw on my shirt, I see her pulling the blanket up as anger floods her face.

"I can't believe you right now. Really? What was this?" She motions to the bed.

As I zip my jeans, I know the last twenty minutes will go down as an asshole move, and the last thing I want is for her to feel like I'm using her. I can only offer honesty.

"It was you and me. Love gets messy sometimes, and right now my love for you is mixed with hurt. I'm trying to find the right way."

"Grays, when you figure it out then you know where I am. Until then, I love you, but I won't wait forever. I need to be the reason you want to be with me. Not because of Rosie or some teenage dream. I need you to want me for how I am right now." Her hand hits her chest and I know I've upset her.

"Wanting you has never been the problem," I say and walk to the door with the confirmation inside of me now hitting me more than ever.

I need to get it together.

Or I may just lose it all.

26

GRAYSON

I'm on my way to Rooster Sin to meet Knox. Driving down the road, I'm very aware that I'm humming a song that is sung by ponies, and I pray to the streaming gods that they release something else that Rosie feels she needs to watch twenty times a day, because this song needs to get out of my head.

For a second, I debate if it's better to have obnoxious lyrics stuck on repeat in my brain or the ongoing reminder that I was an asshole the other night when I went to Brooke's.

I'll take the damn song.

I grunt out a sound as I continue on my way, taking in the warm day, with green fields on both sides of the road. In the distance, I notice someone walking along the road, and as I pass him, I glance in my rearview mirror.

I'd recognize that kid anywhere, the possible thorn to my side when it comes to my sister, and I don't understand why he's walking along the road. If Lucy did something like this, I would lock her bedroom door from the outside.

And maybe it's that thought that makes me slam the brakes then hit reverse. Vaguely in the back of my brain, I remember Coach saying that Drew is a good guy with a rough life. I don't even know what that means, but I hit the brakes again and roll down the window.

He looks up at me, and when he realizes it's me, he looks slightly frightened.

"Get in," I order as I hit the unlock button.

He doesn't answer.

"I said get in." I give him a serious look that I hope gives him the message that I'm not leaving until he is in my car.

Drew looks in both directions, and when he realizes that there's nobody else, he hesitates but then opens the door and slides onto the seat.

The moment he shuts the door, I slam the accelerator again.

"I didn't touch her, I swear." He holds his hands up in surrender.

"That's reassuring, but that's not why you're here. Now tell me, why are you walking in the middle of nowhere?"

He watches me as I drive and shrugs a shoulder. "Oh, a leisurely stroll."

"Right, not buying it. Where's your truck?"

Drew pauses, and I'm not sure if he plans on giving me the truth, but I'm attempting to understand at least. "It's having trouble."

"Okay, so where am I taking you?"

"Anywhere but here." He sighs softly as he looks out the window.

"Fine. Rooster Sin it is, and from there you can walk into town."

Silence fills the car, and for some reason I can't let anything go. It seems to be my new policy on life, but before I can continue my investigation, he speaks.

"She was upset, you know. Lucy, I mean. That's why I drove her home."

I turn my head to him quickly before I look ahead again. "What do you mean?"

"She thought she did something to upset you and that she ruined your life by making you move back here. She told me the other day that she had it all wrong and that you found out you're a dad—well, the whole town is talking about it anyway."

Now things add up a little, as Lucy was quite moody that one day, and I'm relieved that she seems to know that it isn't her fault.

"It's true, I'm a father now." I hear the pride in my voice.

"Your face lights up when you say that. I guess that means you're one of those hands-on types."

"I'd like to think so. What about you? Where are your folks?"

"Mom left when I was a kid, and Dad isn't much of a parent either, he just left six months ago."

Looking to him and I feel sympathetic. "That's rough. And now? What makes you stick around?"

He shrugs a shoulder before he places his hand on the handlebar above his head. "Thought about the army, maybe community college. Coach said he may have a job for me or maybe I could join a construction crew. I'm exploring my options."

"That's why you still hang around the high school, for Coach?" It now all falls into place and I'm even more relieved that I had it all wrong.

"Yeah." He pauses before changing topics. "Is it like they say?"

"What do you mean?"

"The perfect love story. Everyone in town is talking about you and Brooke."

A long exhale draws out of me. "Everyone in town has an opinion about something."

"Didn't you two have a thing way back? Now you're reunited with a kid, can't get much more epic than that."

His choice of words amuses me. "Epic? Sure, let's call it that."

"What's it like? True love and all that. Can't imagine anyone else? Only see a future with her?"

It's exactly like that.

I can't even comprehend someone else, let alone a future without Brooke. If I close my eyes, I swear I see sunflower fields and her smiling at me. It's a commercial of perfect. However, that numb feeling in my chest is still too apparent, the notion she kept a secret.

"It is," I answer simply.

Drew chuckles softly and angles his body to me. "Then why do you look miserable?"

"I'm not miserable, just processing some things."

"Shit, don't wait too long. It takes only a second for something perfect to disappear, and living in regret is more hell than processing something. You have to grab everything you want; it rarely falls into place by itself."

Lines forms on my forehead. "That's a strong piece of advice for a guy who isn't legal drinking age yet."

"Nah, everyone knows if you have everything you want that you don't let it go for even a second. You'd hate to blink and it's gone. You may only get it once."

Pulling up to Rooster Sin, I can't believe how much his words resonate, and I can't help but smile to myself. "I'll be damned, you have some opinions."

"Thanks for the ride," he says as I pull the car into a spot in the lot.

When Drew has his hand on the handle to open, I stop him. "Wait." He looks at me, intrigued. "Listen, go to Olive Owl later. I'll tell my brothers; we may have a job for you."

He smiles at me in appreciation before getting out of the car.

His words dance in my head. *You may only get it once.*

———

KNOX IS SITTING across from me in the booth with a bottle of beer. It's not very busy this afternoon, so for the most part we're alone except for a man sitting at the bar.

"Why did you want to meet? It sounded urgent," I ask.

He looks at me and his strait-laced look is new to me. "Lucy says you and Brooke are still a work-in-progress."

Jeez, nobody is going to leave me alone. "And?"

"You know you did exactly what she did, right? For years, you probably had a hope that somehow you and she would be together again, yet you never acted on it. Instead, you lived your life away from here. Just like she had a hope that you were Rosie's father and never acted on it. Kind of as bad as each other." His hand reaches to something lying next to him on the bench, and he pulls it up then slides the envelope in my direction. "It's for you."

I grab the envelope with my name on it. "I can see that. What is it?"

Knox's expression is peculiar, as if he's about to surprise me and he knows it. "A letter from Dad, for you."

I wasn't expecting him to say that, but it grabs my interest.

"Okay? Why do you have it?" Well, I know why. He was

the closest with Dad, and that's why he probably has this; I just don't understand the reasoning behind it.

He rubs his upper lip with his long finger before grabbing his bottle of beer. "He said I should give it to you when I thought you needed someone to light a fire under your ass... or wait four months after he passed, whichever came first. You qualify for both."

"You read it?"

He shakes his head. "Nope." He pops the P with his lips. "But I can only imagine it has to do with the fact that he chose to buy a house next to Brooke Rivers for a reason. And on that note, I'm heading to the bar." He smirks to himself and pats my back as he passes. "Happy reading."

Looking at the letter, I break the seal and pull out the papers: the legal documents addressed to Brooke and a hand-written letter on top.

Grays,

You know exactly why you're getting this. Brooke may hate me for hiding the document, but that girl has too kind of a heart to hate me for long. And you? Well, guess what? I'm already in another world, so I don't have any awkward family dinners to attend.

So why did I do it? I was too curious about who would be bothering Brooke and for what reason. Some instinct made me do it.

But truly, the answer is simpler than that.

I know you. You are a man of obligations. You would have moved here so fast that the clock wouldn't have had a chance to tick. But you and Brooke needed to find your way back to one another without responsibilities tying you together. And I bet it didn't take long either. I know that, because just the way I loved your mother — who also was my high school girl-friend— I see it in your eyes.

Yeah, I know about every time you snuck Brooke into the house when you were teenagers… that weekend I was away, I knew what was going to happen. The whole damn town probably knew about you two sneaking off at Olive Owl's opening a few years back, and every time someone would mention her name over the years, your eyes would change to something optimistic.

Good news, kid, you don't need to hope. You have it.

Even better, you have it because you found your way back together without knowing your title as maybe dad. I don't know the answer, but I've seen that child's lip quiver in persuasion, and I think I know the outcome of this. I'm also going to take a wild guess that your feathers are slightly ruffled from the fact you're only now finding out.

I loved your mother so damn hard it gave me headaches. I would've given anything if I could have had more time with her. So don't be stubborn, and you get back to the life you were planning in your head for years before this news.

You got your dream job, your city life, years away from Bluetop… but was it everything you wanted? Nah, I bet you were missing something.

She'll love you hard too.

Love ya, kid, even if we never said much.

Dad

P.S. I know you're trying to keep the guys away from Lucy, but it's inevitable… and I never owned a shotgun.

THIS IS TYPICAL. Of course, he gives me his most heartfelt conversation via letter when I have no chance to answer him. When he was alive, he never tried to persuade me that he was always right, but he raises some valid points.

I can only smirk to myself, because today, I've been

schooled by a nineteen-year-old and a ghost. And it's just the kick I need. It's time to snap out of this.

Knox returns and slides into the booth across from me with a knowing look. "All good?"

"Yeah, more than." I take a swig from my beer. "Things are a little clearer."

"Only a little?"

Now I have to grin. "Okay, it's crystal clear, and I need to formulate a plan."

"What would that be?"

"Operation keep Brooke Rivers so close that she'll never escape."

Yeah, I'm done licking my wounds, because I can't risk losing what was there all along—my future with Brooke.

27

BROOKE

L ucy is standing on the other side of the front door after knocking up a storm. It's after dinner and getting dark out, so the light is a mixture of the sunset and the bulb from the porch.

"Everything okay?" I look at her with concern as I stand in front of her in shorts, a t-shirt, and my hair down.

"No, I need you to save me." She barges past me.

"What do you mean?"

"Okay, so I totally had a guy in my room and Grayson has gone a little crazy. Can you go calm him down? You are the only one who can. I'll stay with Rosie until I get the signal that I won't be dead." Lucy speaks with urgency and slight fear, already scooting me back to the door.

Stepping to her, I touch her shoulders. "Okay, okay. Rosie is playing with her dolls. I'll text you when it's safe."

I grab my phone from the table next to the door and rush off.

Great, the last thing the world needs is protective big-brother Grayson. Mix that with him already angry from the last few weeks and whatever poor boy was with Lucy may be roadkill any second.

I run to their house and through the garage, letting myself in at the door.

I'm expecting shouting, but it's the last thing I get.

My body stills as I take in the scene before me. A row of tealight candles on the floor, leading a path through a perfectly quiet house.

Suddenly, I feel like the boy in Lucy's room is all fiction.

I move forward, one step and then the next, as I follow the trail very slowly.

"Grayson?" I call out, and I feel the speed of my heart revving up.

No answer is given, but I feel him here. The journey leads me to the kitchen sink—an odd destination.

Looking around me, I see candles and dimly lit lights in the living room, but no Grayson. I stand there at the sink, lost with what is about to happen, but something tells me it will be okay.

My eye catches one of Rosie's paintbrushes in the sink, which is peculiar, as I could have sworn these were at our house. Turning, I pick it up, and then I feel him. Walking to me, standing next to me, and radiating warm energy.

I can't form words, and I don't need to, as my eyes are occupied by Grayson bringing his own brush to the sink. Then it hits me.

"Just like when we met." How could I not softly smile to myself?

"I fell for you then and never stopped."

My eyes dart up and look to him at my side. "Guess this means there's no teenage boy in a body bag somewhere."

He gives me a puzzled and entertained look, then it dawns on him. "Is that how Lucy got you here?"

"Pretty believable too."

Grayson slants a shoulder with a subtle grin forming. "She has drama class next year for extra credit."

"Oh."

I wait patiently for him to take us in the direction of where this conversation is going.

"I'm sorry, B. I went off track, even when I knew there's nothing else but us."

I swallow and take in the realization that this is our make-up that I hoped would come. "The circumstances are a bit unusual, off track seems understandable." I shrug as my one-tone voice answers.

His hand comes up to cup my face. "You've always been in my dreams, even when I wasn't here. Nothing felt complete, even though I got the things I wanted, but I didn't have you. I was always chasing a fantasy. Weren't you?"

"More than you will ever know," I softly answer in a whimsical tone.

Grayson leans down to tenderly kiss my forehead. "I've been waiting for you to end up in my arms again, and I have it. We have a good thing, and I'm never going to let that go. I don't want to waste any more time."

My eyes peer up to his, and I remind him of what that entails. "That means you can't regret this, or feel like I owe you or I eternally need to say sorry—"

He hushes me by placing his finger on my mouth. "It's you and me, like before, and now even better."

My emerging smile doesn't get a chance to stretch before Grayson slams his mouth onto mine. The brush in my hand falls to the floor as I wrap my arms around him. Our tongues touch, and my entire body comes alive.

Parting, his sinful sounding *mmm* feels like a cold dessert that melts to the touch of a warm spoon.

He takes my hand in his and tows me along, down the hall, and to his home office. The moment he sits on the chair behind his desk, he pulls me to rest on his lap.

"What are you doing?" I smile because I know he has plans.

"Showing you what I've always imagined."

His head indicates to look at the papers on his desk, and I instantly see his designs—a house.

"What's this?"

"Our future is in the house I've been designing, complete with five bedrooms and the kitchen of your dreams."

I snort a laugh. "Five bedrooms?"

He tucks my hair behind my shoulders and the corner of his mouth hitches up. "I have big plans for you, like the expansion of our family after I put a ring on your finger one day."

"Wow, I'm never going to see my feet again," I say before my eyes explore the design some more, and it is absolutely beautiful—modern yet fit for the country.

"We can get some land outside of town near Olive Owl but close enough to school and build on it," he explains.

"I like that idea." My fingers caress the page of what looks like a guest house. "Grayson," I give him my curious tone. "We don't need a guest house."

He laughs at my thought. "That's not a guest house, it's a playhouse for Rosie."

I playfully slap him because it is ridiculous, and next thing I know he'll tell me that he got her an actual live pony.

But I love it all and I kiss him in appreciation. "It's perfect."

His fingers comb through my hair as our eyes get lost in each other.

"We'll go slow—well, not too slow, but we'll be alright, B."

Oh man, I feel happy tears springing up. "How did we end up here? After all these years?"

He kisses my hands that he has clasped in his and then my inner wrist. "We were always going to end up together, because you and I, what we have, it's something right. I fucking love you, and I don't know how to ever stop."

The tears fall, and I don't even care. "I love you, and I promise we are stronger now than before."

"That we are," he whispers before he kisses me again.

Soon he's pulling me close, and I wrap my arms tightly around him as I straddle him until he lifts me and rests me on his desk, and when I'm lying back and he is working his magic on removing my shorts, I notice in the corner of my eye a stack of papers, and then I see it—a brochure for adoption. He wasn't joking. Then a new wave of love hits me, because he doesn't need to adopt his biological child, which means he looked into it before we knew.

We were always in the plan.

EPILOGUE

Grayson- **A few months later**

Waking, my eyes flutter open as I let out a yawn, which only leads to a tiny foot landing in my mouth. Quickly, I realize that Rosie is sprawled out in our bed sleeping. Brooke swears our daughter's love for me was shown the moment when Rosie's foot landed in my face as she slept between us the first time.

It doesn't happen often, only when there are storms—or she's sick or just can't sleep.

Gently sliding the foot to the side, I escape out of bed as I hear the water in the shower and know where to find Brooke.

Clicking the door closed behind me, then more importantly locking it, I take off my t-shirt and boxers as I admire the view of Brooke standing with her back to me under the showerhead.

Joining her, she turns to me with a warm smile forming and her arms reaching out to me. Stepping to her, I plant my hands on her sides and let the water cover my head.

"You're up early," I mumble in a gruff morning voice before kissing that sensitive spot under her ear.

"Mmhmm, and you're hard," she rasps as her hand lands on my cock.

Looking down, I love how my engagement ring looks on her finger when she's gripping me tight. I glance up with a mischievous look.

I yank her flush to me. "This is going to be a good morning."

We know we don't have long, but early mornings are our time before Brooke is off to work and Rosie and Lucy to school.

Standing there, we caress one another with our hands before I turn her, and she rests her hands against the shower wall before bending slightly forward.

Sliding into her and we both enjoy the extra sensitivity of morning sex. We move together until we're both seeing colors behind our eyelids and hold one another up as we both come undone.

Kissing her back, I'm happy this is how we're starting our day today.

She turns in my arms and smiles at me. "Can we just stay like this all day?"

"I would love to, but it's a busy day."

"Mommy!"

Brooke lets her head fall to my shoulder with a sigh. "So it begins. The princess has awoken and needs breakfast."

"Go. I'll be out in a few minutes and I'll take her to preschool."

By the time I make it to the kitchen, Lucy is pouring coffee for herself as she whispers something to Brooke.

I'm still holding out that it isn't boy-related, but since Homecoming is coming up and Lucy has a date, Brooke is taking her dress shopping on the weekend, and I've been ordered to stay clear.

"Morning." I give a steady smile as I reach for the coffee.

"You're getting to-go coffee; I can't be late, I have AP calculus first period." Lucy hands me coffee and a thermos, and I feel like she's telling me off.

"Okay, to-go it is. What about breakfast?" I inquire, to see what regime she has me under today.

Glancing to Rosie, I see she's busy eating her cereal.

"You can have half a power bar." Lucy tosses me a bar, and I chuckle from appreciation.

Lucy has limited driving privileges and an early curfew. Also, no solo rides with Rosie yet, so morning drop-off is still an eventful part of the day.

I walk to Brooke who is busy packing a lunch for work, touching her back. I can't seem to stop touching her.

"Don't forget family dinner tonight." She glances over her shoulder.

"I know. I'll head to Olive Owl after picking up Rosie, and you can get Lucy since you're both cooking. I'm going to stop to check on the construction workers since they're breaking ground on our house this week," I list.

Since Lucy and I spend most of the time with Brooke and Rosie at their house, space is a bit tight. I'm building our dream house, and the day I signed for the land is the day I proposed to Brooke, right there on the grass of our future. When the house is finished, we want to get married in our backyard. But it'll be a while before it's ready. Therefore, family dinners with the entire Blisswood clan are at Olive Owl on a bi-weekly basis.

"Okay." Brooke kisses me quickly before rallying the troops.

———

BROOKE COMES out from the kitchen at the inn and throws her apron to the side. "Hey, I'll be right back. I need to head out to help Kelsey with groceries, uhm, eggs that I forgot to get at the store." She snaps her fingers in the air, and I know this is a cover for something.

"You mean eggs that you can have for free from the chickens here?" I grin because I caught her.

Her evil stare is too sexy, and I'm happy to tease her. She kisses my cheek. "I'll be right back."

Before she gets far, I grab her wrist and spin her in. "If we play our cards right, we can escape for ten minutes later." I flash my eyes at her.

She feigns shock and places her other hand over her mouth. "But it isn't even Thursday."

Date night is Thursdays. The night where we escape to Olive Owl, the fields, the alley behind Rooster Sin, and the good old-fashioned backseat of the car. We've gotten damn creative, since Rosie has no sense of bedroom boundaries.

"Love you," I remind her.

"Love you too, fiancé." She pecks my lips then scurries away, the image of how lucky I am and my future.

"Daddy, can we see the horsy?" Rosie asks as she unpacks her crayons from her little backpack.

"After dinner, okay?"

Lucy looks out the window, as if she's searching for something, before sighing and heading to the kitchen. I'm positive I know who she was watching for. Drew works for us now. Luckily, Drew knows limits, and Lucy's crush is one-sided. It won't stop her from occasionally glancing at him during dinner, though.

Bennett arrives and flops onto a chair, and he looks drained. Knox follows with two bottles of wine and seems to be in an ecstatic mood. He sits next to Bennett, and his overpowering grin sparks my interest as he gets to work on uncorking the wine.

"What's up with you two?" I wonder as I grab a seat across from them.

Knox's brows furrow. "You haven't heard?" His smile widens.

"Heard what?"

"Bennett here had an eventful day." He points his thumb to our brother.

Bennett shakes his head, clearly annoyed.

"What the hell is going on?" I press.

Bennett looks at Rosie blankly, and I have a feeling to get an answer that I need Rosie out of the room. I quickly encourage Rosie to go find Lucy in the kitchen for a pre-dinner snack, then return my focus on my younger brothers.

Knox only chuckles and seems to be taking pleasure in this. "Fun story... so we were sitting here at lunch going over numbers for olive oil bottles, and guess what?"

I'm ready to throw something at him from the suspense.

Knox looks between us and leans back in the chair with a cheeky look. "A woman comes storming in all hell bent, and then she pours a shitload of positive pregnancy tests on the table in front of Bennett. Guess who knocked someone up?"

My mouth falls open, but I can't help but smile at the image as my gaze directs to Bennett who looks like he may murder Knox.

"Thanks for letting me process the news," Bennett sarcastically informs our brother.

"Who did you knock up?" I ask and wait for an answer as all our eyes land on Bennett.

BONUS SCENE: BROOKE

Arriving to the hotel room, Grayson and I are exhausted. Everything that could've gone wrong for the start of a honeymoon, went wrong. The flight to Key West was delayed, the airlines put Grayson and me in seats three rows apart, and the flight attendant spilled orange juice on me without apology.

It's late, and this isn't how I pictured our first night on our honeymoon. We roll our suitcases into the room and look at one another, but I know him and he knows me. Neither of us wants to say it, but we're both thinking it.

Sleep.

It's not like it's our wedding night. We got married back in the spring when the dream house that Grayson built was ready. A small wedding in the garden of our home, with Rosie as a flower girl and Kelsey and Lucy as bridesmaids. We decided to hold off on the honeymoon because it was still the school year and moving a small child and teenager was already work enough. Sure, we had a romantic wedding night in our special room at Olive Owl, but we promised ourselves we would get away for a real honeymoon.

Here we are. It's late August and we were supposed to be on vacation last week, but a hurricane passed through, delaying our trip. Of course, the hurricane missed us, so we could have come anyway. Now my parents are back in Illinois watching Rosie, and Lucy is starting her senior year with supervision from Knox and Bennett.

Grayson steps to me with somber eyes yet a gently assuring smile. "Shower then sleep, or sleep and shower in the morning?" His hands rest on my shoulders.

My head drops and I smile to myself that this is our luck. "Neither option should involve sleep."

"We have all week to make up for it. Plus, the sooner we wake to a new morning, the sooner I get to see you in my favorite bikini." He kisses my forehead, and even tired, his mind is one-track.

Blowing out a breath, I know the right option. "Shower then sleep."

We unzip our suitcases to find everything we need before we head to the bathroom. It's a big bathroom with a rain shower, almost as nice as the one Grayson installed at our home. There is also a tub in the corner, next to doors that must overlook the sea when the sun's up. We keep the lights dim, as bright and loud doesn't really fit our mood right now.

With the shower on, we both step in and instantly find an embrace in one another's arms. We say nothing and let the water cascade down our bodies.

"We will have a good week. The bad luck is behind us," he promises with a low, soft voice.

"This is going to be us, just us, all week. Bars, swimming, lots of sex. Just two carefree adults," I mention as I grab some soap. We've been talking for weeks about which tourist spots we want to check out. I also want to go snorkeling, drink a margarita, and put a dollar up in this one bar. Sure, we will find gifts for the girls. We are on strict orders to bring home a jellyfish, but we informed Rosie that a stuffed animal will have to do.

Grayson glides his hands up my arms, and it causes me to press into his body as I step closer. This feels nice, just being together under warm water and in silence.

Looking up and his eyes meet my own. I still don't understand how I got so lucky. He was my first love, and he is my only love. The years apart from him now feel like they were a test, and since I passed, I get to keep Grayson forever because we found our way back to one another.

After a few more minutes, we turn the water off and dry with towels. I tell Grayson that I need a few more minutes because I just can't flop into bed the way he can. Moisturizing is key!

But as I look through my toiletry bag and my small suitcase with various scraps of clothing, my eye catches on the one item that I picked out on a whim with Kelsey when we went shopping the other week.

I know there's a chance Grayson is already sound asleep, but this is our first night of the honeymoon, and I'm not going to let this be the way our vacation starts.

I grab the scraps of black lace and stockings. I know this isn't my usual bedtime outfit, but it may be exactly what we need to stay up.

———

I THREW the heels on and untied my hair for effect.

Stepping into the bedroom, I internally pray that Grayson hasn't fallen asleep. To my relief, he is sitting up in bed, shirtless and reading a hotel brochure. The moment his eyes look up, his mouth drops, and he throws the brochure to the side.

"I know you're tired but well…"

"I'm not tired anymore, *at all*." He comes to his knees in the middle of the bed, and it feels like he is drinking in the view as his eyes assess me.

My breasts spill slightly out of the bra, and I have stockings and suspenders on. Sure, I throw on silk nighties here and there but never this type of thing. In fact, in all our years, I've never worn something so purposely seductive for after 8pm.

"You like?" I step forward.

He whistles before he hisses a breath. "Fucking gorgeous, now come here. Wait, I'll come to you."

In a flash, he is off the bed and in front of me. He reaches out his fingertips and glides along my arms with a feathery touch. Leaning down, he places a kiss on my cleavage before brushing his lips to the valley of my breasts. Our bodies go flush when his arm wraps around my middle.

"I don't even know where to begin," he growls.

My entire body is melting into a puddle, so he better think quick.

"Touch me where you want," I suggest in a sultry tone.

His fingers pull down the strap of my bra the moment his lips drag along my shoulder to my neck, and my head falls back, offering him everything.

My nipples feel sensitively stiff, and my body eagerly anticipates his next touch.

"Don't move," he whispers, and he kisses me hard yet smooth, confirming that he is going to lead the way.

Our eyes hold as he steps a knee between my legs to part me open. I bite my lip the second he kisses a trail down my body, stopping at my breasts where he lowers the cups and sucks each hard bud, before continuing his quest until he is on his knees before me. Looking down at my husband and I see he is enjoying himself as his nose nuzzles into the fabric of the lace trimming of the stockings.

I giggle from the tickle of his stubble and his teeth biting the suspender.

"You know how to make a grown man go insane," he murmurs, and he pushes my panties to the side before exploring my slit with his fingers.

Instantly, I moan, and my hands brace against his shoulders because he circles and pinches my clit which makes me unstable from pleasure.

"Feel how ready I am for you?" I breathe out as I close my eyes and feel the power of his touch.

"I do, but I need to taste too."

The feeling of his tongue running a line between my folds is pure heaven. He explores me and teases me; my own hands come to cup my breasts because my whole body is alive.

As I glance down, he peers up and he grins against my pussy, then he pulls away, with his mouth covered in my juices.

In one swift move, he picks me up and drops me on the bed. I do my best to lie there in a provocative position, on display for him. I even part my legs extra wide open and touch myself while I watch him strip out of his boxers.

"This is never going to leave my mind." Grayson comes to hover over me, dropping kisses on my breasts then swirling his tongue around my navel. "Soon," he warns. "A baby in here, I want to watch our baby grow inside of you."

I sigh and smile at the same time. "No, we wait," I remind him.

We've talked about this many times, and I do want another baby, but not now. I want to enjoy newlywed life sans morning sickness.

He smiles up at me before sitting back on his knees and stroking himself. "Hands above your head."

I obey and love that we are doing things his way.

"Wider," he demands, and I part my thighs more. He inspects me, and I like that he grins in approval.

But my favorite part is when he moves to enter me, and the moment he is inside me, ecstasy hits. Deep on every pump with our eyes locked. Even when he moves my leg up, we stay intimate.

"God, I love you." His breathing is heavy.

"And I love you—now let me move my hands." I don't wait and move my hands just as his own come to interlace with my fingers, our wedding rings on display.

With every part of us intertwined is the only way we will come together.

And we do.

———

LYING in bed in our afterglow, I rest my head against his chest to listen to the patter of his heart while he strokes my hair.

"You are so sexy, you know that?" he says.

"Good, but it isn't so comfortable." I'm more a shirt and tank kind of girl.

"It's... different but a nice surprise. Is this what every evening of our honeymoon is going to be like?" He's testing his luck.

"I was kind of hoping it would be bikinis and nudity from here on out." I kiss his chest and let my fingers draw patterns on his stomach.

"Also a good plan."

We lie there enjoying the moment, and even though I feel

his mark between my legs, I don't care. I'm not leaving the bed, because I feel the need for the sleep that I avoided. It's hitting me with rage.

"I'm going to do it," he simply states.

I adjust my body so I can study his face. "You mean start the business?"

"Yeah. I've been talking about it for months, but I'm doing it."

I'm so happy for him that he finally made a decision and is starting a contracting business. He'll be using his architecture skills, and Drew is actually good at carpentry, so he thought about hiring him.

"This is wonderful, Grays. Doing something you are passionate about, and it completes the picture."

"The picture?"

"I mean, you get the dream house, the family, the hot wife, and the job. Your dream was in Bluetop all along," I rhapsodize.

He flips me to my back, so I'm trapped under him. "The hot wife and family is all that matters."

"Fine. Everything else is a bonus."

His head dips down to capture my mouth in a kiss. "This is going to be a good week."

"I feel that too." My finger taps the tip of his nose.

"Sleep-ins, breakfast in bed, long walks, romantic dinners, lots of sex."

"Not in that order either."

"We should probably charge up our batteries for tomorrow, as we have priorities to fulfill," he pretends to be concerned but says it casually.

But I'm on to him. "You mean sleep?"

He laughs. "Exactly."

I reach up to cup his face. "I'm happy we made love on our first night of the honeymoon, but fuck, I'm really tired."

He collapses on top of me with a sigh, careful not to crush me. "Thank God, I was scared you were waiting for round two."

I laugh. "No way. It's shut-eye time."

We both shuffle in the bed, and he spoons me from behind.

"Goodnight, Mrs. Blisswood." He kisses my back.

"That's me. Mrs. Grayson Blisswood." I yawn back.

And we fall asleep together just like we always do.

ACKNOWLEDGMENTS

Thank you to you for reading Something Right. This whole series holds a special place in my heart as there are so many little references from another chapter of my life…sadly, minus the hot neighbor who owns a winery is not one of those references.

Thanks to Brittni, for being the first to read. It is a big help and part of my process.

Lindsay, thanks for editing and I'm so excited to be diving into a new series with you!

A certain Belgian bookstagrammer gets credit for helping me pick our Grayson. .

My ARC team and bookstagrammers for sharing, can't do any release without you.

Lindsey at Lily Bear Design Co., thank you for the amazing special edition covers.

Autumn, my publicist rock. Always thank you!

A big thank you to the essentials of my life, husband, kid, and coffee. We did it again!

Made in United States
Troutdale, OR
12/29/2023

16550229R00137